MW01716277

GIRL WITHOUT A CHANCE

(A Tara Strong Mystery—Book 1)

Rylie Dark

Rylie Dark

Bestselling author Rylie Dark is author of the SADIE PRICE FBI SUSPENSE THRILLER series, comprising six books (and counting); of the CARLY SEE FBI SUSPENSE THRILLER series, comprising six books (and counting); of the MIA NORTH FBI SUSPENSE THRILLER series, comprising six books (and counting); of the MORGAN STARK FBI SUSPENSE THRILLER series, comprising five books (and counting); of the HAILEY ROCK FBI SUSPENSE THRILLER series, comprising five books (and counting); and of the TARA STRONG MYSTERY series, comprising five books (and counting).

An avid reader and lifelong fan of the mystery and thriller genres, Rylie loves to hear from you, so please feel free to visit www.ryliedark.com to learn more and stay in touch.

ISBN: 978-1-0943-3055-6

BOOKS BY RYLIE DARK

TARA STRONG MYSTERY
GIRL WITHOUT A CHANCE (Book #1)
GIRL WITHOUT A HOME (Book #2)
GIRL WITHOUT A TRACE (Book #3)
GIRL WITHOUT A NAME (Book #4)
GIRL WITHOUT A PRAYER (Book #5)

HAILEY ROCK FBI SUSPENSE THRILLER
BEHIND YOU (Book #1)
BESIDE YOU (Book #2)
AFTER YOU (Book #3)
WATCHING YOU (Book #4)
JUDGING YOU (Book #5)

SADIE PRICE FBI SUSPENSE THRILLER
ONLY MURDER (Book #1)
ONLY RAGE (Book #2)
ONLY HIS (Book #3)
ONLY ONCE (Book #4)
ONLY SPITE (Book #5)
ONLY MADNESS (Book #6)

MIA NORTH FBI SUSPENSE THRILLER
SEE HER RUN (Book #1)
SEE HER HIDE (Book #2)
SEE HER SCREAM (Book #3)
SEE HER VANISH (Book #4)
SEE HER GONE (Book #5)
SEE HER DEAD (Book #6)

CARLY SEE FBI SUSPENSE THRILLER
NO WAY OUT (Book #1)
NO WAY BACK (Book #2)
NO WAY HOME (Book #3)
NO WAY LEFT (Book #4)

NO WAY UP (Book #5)
NO WAY TO DIE (Book #6)

MORGAN STARK FBI SUSPENSE THRILLER
TOO LATE (Book #1)
TOO CLOSE (Book #2)
TOO FAR GONE (Book #3)
TOO LOST (Book #4)
TOO BROKEN (Book #5)

CHAPTER ONE

"You know, that sun is looking pretty low," Adriana said, shivering lightly. She couldn't help but worry as she hugged her arms against herself.

Krystin looked and checked the reflection in the lake.

"We'll set up the tent quickly," she said. "How hard can it be, right? We'll be tucked up safely in our sleeping bags before the monsters come out."

Adriana shuddered, getting out of the car. She wondered for the hundredth time if it had been a good idea to come with Krystin on this camping trip. She loved her friend, but all her ideas usually led to trouble.

Adriana followed Krystin as she walked around to the back of the car and opened the trunk. The heavy bag containing the tent was there, waiting for them.

"My brother said not to damage it. If we manage to lose any stakes or unravel any guy ropes, he said he'll go into my room and break one thing at random for each bit of damage to the tent."

Adriana reached for the straps of the bag and hefted it, managing to lift it down to the ground and drop it with a heavy clunk. There was a metallic rattling of poles and stakes as it landed.

They heaved it with a joint effort, throwing the whole kit onto the ground with a thud and rattle and stopping to catch their breaths. Adriana put her hands on her hips and turned her head in all directions from their car.

"This is the best spot ever," Krystin said.

They had found a secluded camping area just out of sight of the lake, back in the trees. There was only one other camper in this part of the park, far enough away that their lights were just a dim glow.

"I love this side of the lake," she went on. "The mountain kind of starts not far from here and the trees are thicker. It feels like we're in the middle of nowhere. Like a real camping trip."

"This *is* a real camping trip," Adriana said, annoyed. "We're sleeping in a tent."

"You know what I mean," Krystin said, rolling her eyes. "Like, s'mores and campfires and talking to boys under the light of the moon."

Adriana looked around at the darkening horizon.

"Are you sure this is safe? There's only one other camper over there – and it's so far away."

"It should be fine," Krystin shrugged. "We can go over there if we need help."

Adriana sighed and tried to be calm. It was Krystin's birthday, after all.

"This is the best eighteenth birthday trip anyone has ever planned," Krystin giggled. "And we haven't put the tent up yet."

"It's going to be even better," Adriana promised.

She smiled for the first time as she walked to the backseat of the car and pulled out a sports duffel bag that normally held tennis rackets and gym clothes—now hiding bottles of beer.

"You are so bad," Krystin said, grinning.

"Let's get this tent set up," Adriana grinned. "And be glad that there's no one out here to check if we're underage."

"Where do the poles go?" Adriana asked, experimentally lifting the tent canvas in a few places. "And what are those sheets for?"

"I don't know. Maybe to keep us dry while we put the tent up in case it rains?" Krystin said.

"I think the poles kind of click together like this," Krystin said, spotting two metal ends that looked like they fit together and joining them with a satisfying clink. "Then we just have to figure out where to put them."

"Through these loops, I think," Adriana said. "Or maybe we use the rope to tie the pole to the tent? No… no, I think it's these loops and tubes."

Adriana started to work, increasingly frustrated, trying to figure it out as Krystin joined in. With one pole safely through the outer tubing of the tent, they stared at the piece of canvas flat on the ground.

"Now what?" Krystin asked. "It's, like, not going up, or whatever."

"I don't know," Adriana said.

"Didn't you ask your brother how it worked?"

"I told you what an asshole he was being," Adriana exclaimed, throwing her hands up in the air. "Maybe we should have come here earlier. I didn't think it was going to take this long."

"We're going to run out of light soon," Krystin acknowledged, looking up.

Adriana noticed with a pang of fear that the sun had already dropped far enough that she couldn't see it beyond the trees. There was just an orange glow as a promise that it still existed over there, and that wasn't going to last long.

"Crap. Maybe we should have asked someone for help," Adriana said doubtfully. She looked around. "Where's the light from that other camper?"

"They must have turned it off," Krystin said. "Maybe they went to bed already. Or drove away or something."

"Maybe there's something online…"

Adriana grabbed her cell phone and started tapping the screen. A shiver ran down her spine, full of unease and trepidation.

"Perfect. There's no signal out here."

Then Adriana froze, mid-step. The hair rose on the back of her neck.

"Did you hear something?" she asked.

Krystin looked around, nervous.

And then Krystin straightened up. She must have heard it too.

It sounded to Adriana like…the distant sound of someone screaming.

Adriana looked back at the car, wondering if they should just leave.

"Krystin--" Adriana started.

But her warning was lost completely as a figure burst out of the woods in front of them, emerging from the thicker trees into the wider space they had chosen.

She was screaming, screaming something incoherent at the top of her lungs, her arms flailing beside her pale face as she ran headlong toward them.

"Oh, my God!" Krystin screamed, leaping toward Adriana as if they could have some safety in numbers, or to hide behind her friend, or maybe to defend her.

Adriana grabbed at her, pulling her close, as the woman continued to run right at them. She was saying something – something that wasn't quite clear – something lost in the screaming. The same phrase, it sounded like, over and over again.

"HEEZOWINTAKULMEEEE! HEEZOWINTAKULMEEEE!"

She ran right to Adriana and Krystin's feet and fell, tumbling right onto the ground, reaching out to clutch at their feet. They girls screamed again and jumped back, out of her reach.

"Oh my God, oh my God," Krystin said over and over again. The woman – her hand was bloodied. She was dirty and panting for breath like she'd run so far and so fast she couldn't take another step. She was sobbing into the dirt.

Adriana's brain rearranged the sounds she had heard into words. Words she didn't want to hear. Words that had her staring up at the tree line and whimpering, grabbing Krystin's arm.

And then, the woman, desperate, looked up and screamed right at them:

"He's going to kill me!"

CHAPTER TWO

Tara checked that her radio was on, and pulled it away from her Deputy Sheriff uniform to see the switch on the side.

"It's on," Glenn chuckled, as he drove them slowly down the back streets of Wyatt, Colorado. "There's just nothing happening."

Tara sighed. "I was just making sure," she said quietly.

The town was almost silent at this time of day, right at the beginning of their shift. The only people stirring were those who worked on the land - mountain rangers and park guides and campsite staff.

Glenn grinned at her.

"Sorry, you're stuck with me on the drunkard beat," he said. "If we don't find Billy Westfoot in one of these alleys, you can start to get excited that maybe he wandered off somewhere and died."

Tara stared at him, shaking her blonde ponytail off her shoulder and behind her head.

"I don't want Billy Westfoot to die," she said. "Though the way he drinks, it's probably coming sooner or later no matter who wants it. I just want a bit of excitement. Something more important than tracking down the local drunk every time he doesn't come home at night."

Glenn braked, the patrol car coming to an abrupt stop.

"Found him," he says. "I think I see him breathing. Anyway, aren't you looking forward to the excitement of dinner with your folks tonight?"

Tara ignored what had to be a joke – since dinner with her parents was rarely exciting, and if her sister was there, usually cause for dismay – and leaned forward to look past him out of the car window. She spotted the familiar form of Billy slumped in the alley. He was sitting up with his back against the brick wall of one of the local bars, his arm over a crate and his head pillowed on it. He was asleep.

He was so drunk that he fell asleep in the alley, like he did at least once a week, and this was the job Tara had signed up for when she wanted to protect and serve her county. Even if it wasn't very exciting, it was necessary. Without her and Glenn coming out here every Monday morning to find him, Billy Westfoot probably would be in trouble.

She took hold of her radio as Glenn got out of the car. "Dispatch, we have a ten-ninety-eight. Billy looks like he spent the night in the elements again. Deputy Grayson is looking him over now."

"Ten-four on that, Deputy Sheriff Strong," the reply crackled back over the radio. "I'll call Mrs. Westfoot and let her know."

Tara put the radio back in its cradle, glancing up toward the two figures. Glenn turned and gave her a thumbs up: Billy Westfoot was fine, probably still drunk from the night before like he always was. Glenn's dark curls caught the morning light filtering down the alley as the sun finally rose high enough to hit him, reminding her of just how early it was. Behind him, framed between the gap of the two buildings, the mountain rose high and hazy in the distance.

She got out of the car on her side, stretching out her back a little, and joined Glenn.

"I'm fine here," Billy slurred, trying to push Glenn's helping hand away. "Jus' leave me."

"Billy, you've got to get on home," Glenn said, trying to persuade him gently. Billy Westfoot was a big man; he had maybe a hundred pounds on Glenn. Tara knew from experience that it would take both of them to get the habitual drunk up and into the car if he didn't want to go. "Your wife called us in a panic again this morning. She thought you'd gone and got yourself lost or something."

"Come on, Billy," Tara said, trying a more no-nonsense tone. "You have to get up now. We can't leave you here, you know that. Either we annoy each other for the next hour and then you come, or you just come anyway and cut out the middle part."

Billy heaved a sigh, his whole heavyset frame wobbling. "She's a nag, isn't she?"

Glenn shot a look of dark, mischievous amusement in Tara's direction. Coupled with his curly dark hair and the somewhat elfin set to his features, it made him look like a dark sprite there to cause her trouble. "A nag, you say, Billy? You sure you want to use that word?"

"I swear to God," Tara muttered under her breath so Billy couldn't hear her, looking back toward the mouth of the alley and the car they had left undefended. She pretended she was checking it over just in case someone was trying to steal it, but she knew Glenn had known her long enough to realize that she was actually seething. She needed a moment to calm down and put her professional face back on, so she could smile at Billy like she hadn't heard him.

"All women nag," Billy went on, and Tara had to walk away toward the car. There were certain things she had a hard time tolerating, and discrimination of any kind was one of them.

Dealing with this kind of small-town misogyny was bad enough, but doing it in hot pursuit of lost drunks and cats up in trees was the injury added to the insult. Not for the first time and almost definitely not for the last, Tara's frustration took her to thoughts of her sister. Jessy Strong had joined law enforcement just the same way that Tara had, but the oldest Strong child had already managed to get herself a position as Sheriff in the next county over. Not only that, but it was a bigger county, and they had actual crimes to deal with on a daily basis. Exciting things happened over there. Not here.

Tara was going to spend thirty years of her life, if she was lucky, getting called darling and heckled as a nag by the drunks, domestic abusers, and petty small-time thieves of Wyatt, and then she was going to retire early just to get out of the place, and Jessy was going to keep getting accolades and her name in the paper.

Not that being in the paper bothered Tara. But just getting her hands on a real case would make a nice break from the monotony. Just once. She didn't want to wish bad things on the town. But she wanted to do something that mattered – something that made it feel like her life had been time well spent.

"That's it," Glenn was saying behind her, and Tara glanced over her shoulder to see Billy Westfoot shuffling along, one hand on the brickwork for support. She opened the door to the backseat and stood aside, watching the sky and the mountain beyond. It looked peaceful up there.

Billy got in, Glenn holding his head to make sure he didn't hit it, and Tara closed the door. She looked at Glenn, who stood about an inch taller than she did, and he grinned.

"All in the glamorous day's work of a deputy in Edgar County," he said.

Tara couldn't quite hold back her smile of amusement at how he'd managed to figure out what she was thinking, but she stifled it quickly. She put on a faux stern look befitting his superior.

"Oh, come on, T," he said, patting her on the shoulder. "Maybe it won't catch any headlines, but it's still important work." He moved around to the driver's seat and got in, leaving her to walk to the passenger side.

She hesitated before she got in, knowing that as soon as she did, she had to put her professional face back on. Drunkard or not, Billy Westfoot was a civilian, and she had to act like her role.

"I know it is," she murmured, reminding herself of that very fact. Maybe they weren't busting up drug rings or solving murders of young couples on lovers lanes, but that was alright, wasn't it? They were making a difference. They really were. Every time one of the citizens in Wyatt stopped Tara when she was out grocery shopping, wanting to thank her for helping them out with something or another, she remembered it.

She got back into the car and found that professional face slipping back on easily as she glanced at Billy Westfoot's dozing form in the rear view mirror.

They were ten minutes down the road, another five still from the Westfoot house, when Tara's cell phone rang. She grabbed it out of her pocket and checked the caller ID: Sheriff Braddock.

"Sheriff," she said, answering the call.

"Tara, where are you right now?" Braddock asked immediately, doing away with all formalities.

Tara glanced in the rearview mirror at their passenger. "Just transporting Billy Westfoot back home."

"Take you long?"

"Five minutes."

"I need you right away – tell Glenn to step on it."

Tara gestured to Glenn, making a pushing gesture, and he put his foot down further on the accelerator. "What's going on, sir?"

"I've got a case here that I need my second-in-command on," he said. "A serious case. Get down to the hospital as soon as you can."

"The hospital?" Tara repeated, glancing at Glenn as he glanced back. This did sound serious. Her mind instantly went to all the senior citizens in town who might be in physical trouble, all the workers who might have been caught up in some kind of industrial accident. She even thought of her parents, though Braddock had called it a case, and she couldn't imagine they'd be the ones hurt if that's how he'd phrased it.

“Yes,” Braddock said. “This is bigger than anything we’ve handled before. Just get here fast and I’ll explain as we go.”

Tara hung up when the Sheriff did, looking at Glenn. “We’ve got to get there right now,” she said. “It’s a real case.”

And though she was afraid that something terrible might have happened, for just a moment, a flare of excitement lit up her chest.

Something was happening.

CHAPTER THREE

Tara rushed through the main doors of the hospital, looking around. One of the nurses behind the main desk, an older woman who had treated Tara the last time she was here as a teenager with a broken wrist, hurried towards her.

"Deputies," she said, greeting Tara and Glenn at the same time. "The Sheriff told me to bring you through as soon as you got here."

"Who is it?" Tara asked the nagging question that had been plaguing her during the breakneck rush to get here. She knew everyone in town – she'd grown up here, and then served the community in her role as Deputy Sheriff. If she didn't know them to speak to, she at least knew who everyone was, some snippet of their story. If it was someone from further out in the county, she might not be as familiar with them, but there was a good chance it was someone she had met during her work.

"She's not local," the nurse replied, glancing around the waiting room as she walked as if to tell them that there were too many prying ears. "Come on, I'll take you right to her."

Tara raced behind the nurse's quick steps, Glenn coming up behind her. Eyes turned in their direction, following the two deputies who were obviously in a hurry to attend to one of the patients here. Tara ignored them. She'd gotten used to being stared at – it came with the uniform. What mattered right now was finding out what was going on.

They turned down a quieter hall, and the nurse glanced over her shoulder to check how close Tara was. "All we know for sure at the moment is her identity," she said. "She was carrying ID documents and the photographs match up, and we were able to pull her medical records. Her name is Miley Piper."

"Anything in her history we need to know about?" Tara asked.

"Nothing at all," the nurse said. "She's barely needed any medical attention since she was born. There's a chance her family didn't have insurance and she avoided coming into hospitals, but as far as her record, she's had a pretty healthy life."

Tara nodded, storing that information away. The next thing she would want to know would be about Miley Piper's criminal record, but that wasn't something the nurse could answer. She filed it for now. "Why is she here?"

The nurse turned around fully, walking backwards, to give her a dark look for a moment. "Something terrible has happened to that girl. I don't know what, exactly, but she was terrified when she came in. Exhausted. She's run until she couldn't run anymore."

Up ahead, Tara saw the tall, white-haired figure of Sheriff Braddock leaning against the wall. He was next to the door to a private room, and Tara wasn't at all surprised when the nurse slowed down.

"Thank you, nurse," Sheriff Braddock nodded to her gratefully. "Tara, Glenn. This is a tough one. She's traumatized. Won't talk to me. She won't talk to Glenn, either."

"How do you know that?" Tara asked, looking at Glenn with wide eyes. Had he been here before against her knowledge?

"She's skittish around men," the Sheriff explained. He shook his head, blue eyes wrinkling in his tanned skin. "I hate to think what's happened to her. She seems better around the nurses, so I think you ought to go in there alone to talk to her."

"Okay," Tara nodded. It was a lot of responsibility to shoulder, but she had been waiting for that. This was her opportunity to step up. And besides, she was Deputy Sheriff – just one rung below the Sheriff himself. This was the kind of task a deputy had to take on. "Do we have any information at all, to get started?"

"She showed up bloody and dirty, and she was screaming about someone trying to kill her," Sheriff Braddock said grimly. "She ran right into the campsite up by the lake – a couple of teenage girls up there found her. Other than that, and her name, we have nothing."

Tara nodded. "Alright." She squared her shoulders. After a moment's thought, she unbuckled her gun holster and handed it to Glenn, who easily clipped it onto his own belt as if it was a move they had practiced. No need to spook the young woman even further by showing her a deadly weapon.

She faced the doorway and took a moment. She glanced at Sheriff Braddock. He gave her an encouraging smile and a nod. Tara reminded herself that if she wasn't up to the task, Braddock wouldn't have put her forward for it. He knew what she was capable of, and she trusted his judgement.

Tara reached for the door handle, opened it, and stepped through, putting a friendly smile on her face which she hoped would hide any nervousness.

"Hi," she said softly, seeing a wide-eyed face looking back at her from the bed. The young woman lying in it looked frail and fragile, as people often did in hospital beds. She was redheaded, her long hair nestled against the pillow and framing her face, which was pale and marked with scratches around the periphery. Tara didn't know whether they came from branches of trees or from the fingernails of her attacker, but the overall effect was pitiful. The rest of her body was hidden under the white covers of the hospital bed, and a finger on one hand was caught in a clip hooking her up to a monitoring machine.

"Hello," the young woman – Miley, Tara remembered – said cautiously. She looked worried, glancing back at the door as if she was afraid someone else could burst through at any moment.

"It's just me for now," Tara said reassuringly. She sat down in the chair beside the bed, uncomfortable and cold plastic, but tried not to show it on her face. "My name is Deputy Sheriff Strong, but you can call me Tara. What's your name?"

"Miley," the girl replied, which at least meant that she knew who she was and she was willing to be truthful about it.

Tara smiled wide, as if she'd just been given a gift. All the while, she was trying to get as much information from the girl as she could. She wasn't a girl, really – a woman, probably in her early twenties. She just looked so small and vulnerable in that bed.

She was beautiful, too. The kind of beauty that you could be jealous of. The kind of beauty, Tara thought darkly, that could make you a target for a man who didn't like to accept no for an answer.

"Miley, you gave everyone a bit of a fright," Tara began, then realized she didn't want to make the victim feel guilty and tried to backtrack a little. "What we're all worried about is you – about what happened to you. We want to make sure you're alright."

"I'm alright now," Miley said, her voice little more than a ghost. She looked down and picked at the sleeve of her hospital gown with one slim, pale finger. "So long as…"

"So long as you're safe in here?" Tara guessed. "You're worried about someone coming after you."

Miley nodded, her face pinched tight with fear and sadness, not meeting Tara's eyes.

"Don't worry," Tara said. "Right now, my partner and the Sheriff are standing right outside your door, and I'm here. And we'll make sure someone stays there to watch over you all the time you're here."

Miley's eyes dropped to the blanket on the bed again, as if she was unwilling to commit. She didn't say anything.

"Do you want to tell me what happened to you?" Tara asked.

She felt impatient. She wanted answers. Glenn would have been better at this interview, she was pretty sure – but if the girl was uneasy around men, then Tara was really the only person who could do this. She watched Miley pick at a tiny loose thread on the sheet that covered her, her eyes unfocused, and tried not to sigh with frustration.

Tara tried to remind herself the girl had been through something horrible. Miley was still scared. She probably needed more reassurance.

What would Tara want if she was in her position?

"Once you go home, I'm sure we can arrange something to make sure no one can get to you," Tara said, trying to bribe her. "We can have a car outside your house. Would that make you feel better?"

Miley nodded, glancing up shyly. "All the time?" she asked. "No… no breaks?"

"All the time," Tara nodded. She paused before going on. Miley was scared of men – that meant more than likely her attacker was male. "You know, Miley, it would be really useful if we knew who to watch out for. Who you're scared of. If you tell us who it is, we can make sure that he gets put behind bars. That way, we can protect you even better."

Miley bit her lip. "Him," she whispered, so Tara had to lean in closer to listen.

"Who is he?" Tara asked.

"He was… he was going to…"

"To kill you?" Tara suggested gently. "That's what you were screaming when you ran out of the trees."

Miley's green eyes closed for a moment, a single tear escaping one of them. She opened them again but focused on the blanket. Tara was losing her again. She shouldn't have interrupted. She tried to remind herself of something – that Miley was a person, a real human, not a 'case.' She imagined it was her own sister sitting there, and the answer became clear.

Tara reached out and gently touched her hand where it lay on the bed, wanting to comfort her. She didn't say anything or press her until she was ready.

"He was going to kill me," Miley confirmed, her voice straining between a whisper and a hoarse whine.

"Can you tell me what happened?" Tara asked, keeping her tone as gentle as possible. "Start at the beginning – at before you met him."

"I was just walking down the street," Miley said. Her voice was plaintive, as if she wanted to ask why such a thing had happened to her, to proclaim that it wasn't fair. "I was walking on my own, on my way home, and this car pulled up beside me."

"Do you remember anything about the car?" Tara asked eagerly. This could be an extremely good lead. "The make and model, or the color?"

"No," Miley said, shaking her head. "It was all so fast. I saw the headlights – they were so bright, I couldn't make out anything else." She crumpled a little, as if Tara's eager question and the fact she couldn't answer it were disappointing to the point of tears.

"You're doing really well, don't worry." Tara said, giving her a moment before asking her next question. "It was nighttime?" That was a good point to establish.

"Yes," Miley nodded. "I was there and then the next thing I knew, he grabbed me. I tried to scream and something was over my mouth. I tried to fight him but he hit me over the head."

"Have you told the nurses this?" Tara asked. Getting evidence and the girl's story was one thing, but the other important point was to make sure that she had received the right medical treatment. A blow to the head could be serious. Could leave her with lasting damage, especially if it wasn't treated properly as soon as possible.

Miley nodded slowly. "They asked me if I had any injuries."

"That's good," Tara said, and smiled. She squeezed Miley's hand lightly. "You're doing really good."

"After I woke up, I was in a house," Miley said. "Or a cabin, or something. I don't know."

"Okay," Tara nodded. "Were you tied up?"

"Yes," Miley said. She looked down at her hands as if to confirm for herself that it had really happened. There were faint red marks there on her wrists. Rope burns, but not deep ones. "I didn't try to fight. I asked him why I was tied up and he said it was so I couldn't run."

Tara seized on this opportunity to get more evidence about this man who had kidnapped her. "What did he look like?" she asked, deliberately keeping her voice as soft as possible.

"I didn't see him," Miley said, shaking her head. "I had a blindfold on."

"What about his voice? Did he have an accent?" Even though she was pressing, she kept up that same tone, not wanting Miley to retreat again at the thought she was letting Tara down with her lack of answers.

Miley thought back, but shook her head slowly. "He just sounded like he was from around here."

A local, then, possibly. Though she wasn't sure whether Miley was familiar enough with Wyatt itself to know the particular idiosyncrasies of dialect and accent that residents had, being somewhat isolated from other settlements for so long. Maybe she only meant he was from this general area – this state, or this half of the country – who knew. Tara stored this away for now. She wanted to get through the whole story before she pushed Miley harder. She was clearly hanging on the edge. She looked so tired and worn, and her face pinched with pain and fear and winced with every question. They could drill down into serious details in a later interview.

"What happened then?"

"He kept me there overnight and for the whole of the next day," she said. "I had the blindfold on all the time. And then he untied me."

"Why?" Tara asked, blurting it out before she could stop herself. What a strange thing for a killer to do – especially if he really intended to kill her. The kidnapping was bad enough and he must have known that if Miley escaped, she would be able to potentially lead to his conviction.

"He said it was time for me to eat my last meal," she said. Her hands were shaking even where they lay on the bed. "That was when I knew. He was going to kill me. He said he made it special because it was the last thing I would ever eat. He took off my blindfold and told me not to look at him and then he backed out of the room and left me. There was a tray of food and I was so hungry, but…"

Tara nodded encouragingly. "You didn't want to eat it?"

Miley shook her head. "I thought it might be poisoned."

"That's a reasonable thing to think," Tara agreed. "What did you do?"

"I took the covers off the bed and I wrapped them all around my arms and body, and held them in front of my face. The window was locked, so I took a run up from the far side of the room and jumped through it," Miley said. "And then I just ran, and I didn't stop running."

Tara took a deep breath. She'd been through something awful. "You've been so brave," she said. "We're going to find the man who did this to you so you don't need to be afraid. Is there anything you can tell me about where you were? Do you remember where you ran from?"

Miley shook her head. "I don't know how long I was running for, but it was dark," she said. "I could barely see anything. I just ran and ran – I didn't know where I was going, but I tried to go in a straight line. I thought eventually I would come across someone else or a road or another house. I was so scared I just kept going. I don't even think I ever looked to one side or the other."

Tara felt sympathy, but also frustration. She must have been so terrified to not even know where she was running. At the same time, though, more information would really help. "What about when you were inside? Do you remember anything that might help us figure out where you were?"

Miley shook her head slowly, but then stopped abruptly. "I heard water," she said, as if it was coming to her as a bit of divine inspiration. "Running water, nearby. I heard it through the window and when I ran it was louder."

"Running water?" Tara asked. Her head was already flashing through a mental map of the area above the lake, the mountains, the woods. There were smaller lakes and rivers up there. Whenever someone local spoke of 'the lake,' they meant the big one – but there were many more. "Like a river or like a lake lapping at the shore?"

"I…" Miley hesitated. "I don't know. Just water."

She had been turning something over in her hand, Tara realized suddenly – not playing with the loose thread on the blanket at all. There was a flash of something metallic, something that caught Tara's eye.

"What are you holding?" she asked, keeping her tone curious and light instead of accusatory. "Is that a piece of jewelry?" It was the best guess she could think of. What would someone hold onto at a time like this? A ring, a necklace, a gift from a family member?

"It's what he gave to me," Miley whispered, and Tara's blood went cold.

"He gave you something?" Tara asked, and when Miley nodded, Tara bit her lip to hold herself back a moment before continuing. Softly, she reminded herself – don't push too hard. "May I see it?"

There was a beat, a moment in which Tara thought she had failed after all and Miley didn't trust her enough. But then there was a quick movement of her fingers and she lifted the item up, showing it to Tara on her open, trembling palm.

It was a dog tag – a single tag, blank on this side. The edges were well-worn, as though they had been turned over and over in someone's hand for years. Slowly, Tara reached out, making eye contact with Miley first to check it was still alright before picking it up.

"Is it okay if I take this and show it to my colleagues?" Tara asked, turning it over. The other side of the tag chilled her to the bone, making the hairs stand up on the back of her neck. It wasn't a name and ID code like she had expected. It was just a number, apparently stamped into the metal with some kind of carved tool. A number five.

Five what?

"Yes," Miley said, her voice a ghost still. "I don't want it."

Tara nodded approvingly as if Miley had achieved something amazing. She wasn't sure how the girl had held onto it through her initial examination, with the rest of her clothes being taken as evidence to be checked over by the lab, but at least they had this tag now. "You've done really well, Miley. I want you to get some rest now, but we'll come and talk to you again soon. Is that okay?"

Miley nodded. "Yeah," she said, giving Tara a smile as if she was a friend promising to visit again next week.

Tara stood up, looking down at her with another flare of pity. What she had been through was the kind of thing that could take a long time to get over.

But Tara could help with that.

"I'll see you later, then," she said, moving towards the door with a smile.

She could catch the man who had kidnapped and threatened to kill her – and then Miley would be able to sleep better at night.

There was a creep out there somewhere with a home or cabin near water, and Tara was going to find him before he could frighten or hurt anyone else.

CHAPTER FOUR

Tara stood on top of the hill and shaded her eyes, looking left to right across the horizon. Not that it helped much. Even up here, it was hard to see through the trees.

"We've got a lot of ground to cover," Glenn said grimly.

"I know," Tara said. She was starting to feel a bit less optimistic herself. She had marched out of that hospital room feeling determined, like she was going to go out there and have the would-be killer in cuffs by the end of the day. But now, actually standing on ground near the lake and seeing how vast it was, and knowing there was a chance that Miley had actually run for the better part of a whole night and day – a higher than good chance, given her physical condition – she was feeling a little less sure.

The problem was the scale. There were lakes all around this area, smaller bodies of water too, and they were all fed by rivers and streams. A house or cabin near water in the woods – it was nowhere near precise enough to give them a good idea of where to start. And the manpower assigned to the case was, basically at this point, Tara and Glenn. Sheriff Braddock had gone back to headquarters to see if he could scare up some help from other counties, while one of their other deputies was on Miley's door.

"Where do you want to start?" Glenn asked. That was to his credit, Tara thought. Instead of wanting to give up or turn away, he saw the scale of the task and simply rolled up his sleeves.

"I don't know," Tara sighed. She rubbed her forehead. A shiver ran down her back, thinking about it.

"What's wrong?" Glenn asked, picking up on her unease.

"I just…" Tara paused, trying to put the feeling into words. She spread her hands to indicate the whole of the horizon. "Somewhere out there, in our community, there's a killer. Or someone who tried to be a killer, at least."

"Yeah." Glenn paused, looking out where her hands had swept as if there was a chance they might spot him from here. "Yeah, it's..."

"A lot," Tara supplied. She chuckled ruefully. "I feel like an idiot. I'm always saying I want something more exciting to happen, but..."

"But when it does, you realize someone has to get hurt in order for that to be the case," Glenn said. He was pretty good at psychoanalyzing her, it turned out. He always had been.

Tara nodded. "I'm... I don't know. Kind of ashamed, I guess. I wished for something to happen, and now this poor girl went through all this trauma, nearly died, all for me to get my exciting case."

"You didn't make it happen," Glenn told her. "But now that it has, let's not waste it."

Tara nodded. "You're right. Let's start by following her path back through the trees. She was found there, so if we head back in roughly a straight line, it looks like the nearest properties are those over by the northwest shore of the lake."

"Then let's go," Glenn said, turning immediately and heading back to where they had parked the car.

They drove around the side of the lake, quickly coming up to the first properties – lakeside cabins. The cabins fell into a few different categories. Some were rentals, which meant they were going to need to figure out if anyone had checked out right before Miley ran out of the woods. Some were owned by locals, either as seasonal homes or places to retreat on special occasions or weekends. Others still were owned by out-of-towners who would come in on holiday weekends. It was late summer, which meant it was a crapshoot whether anyone would be here on vacation still or already back home.

They parked outside the first place. It was frustrating – the distance between the cabins could be so long that there was no making it on foot, not in any kind of timely fashion. They couldn't split up and tackle more properties at the same time. Tara could have finished three visits driving between them before Glenn would have been able to walk to a second cabin. They had to do it together, but it just felt like one more delay on top of how long the whole process was going to take.

"We have to try not to alert everyone to what went on," Tara said. "The less chance he has to get a head start on us, the better."

"Right," Glenn nodded. His brown curls caught the light filtering through the trees as they walked towards the front of the lakeside property, the sound of the water to their right a constant. It was a lovely day – the kind of day that was perfect for owning a cabin by a lake. It chilled Tara to the core to think that terrible things could happen on perfect days like this. "We'll have to be subtle."

Tara gave him a significant look which meant it was time to be quiet about their planning, just in case they were overheard, and then stepped forward to knock three times on the door of the house. It was painted a bright merry yellow, well-maintained, with flowers blooming in pots beside the door. There was a good bet, at least, that the people who lived here did so year-round.

The door opened to reveal an older woman in a yellow daisy-patterned apron, looking up at them with flour-dusted hands as if surprised to see them. This was a fairly regular occurrence – most people weren't expecting the Sheriff's department to show up, and when they did, it often wasn't for good reasons.

"Can I help you?" the woman asked, in tones that slightly suggested she hoped that she couldn't.

"I'm Deputy Sheriff Strong, ma'am, and this is Deputy Grayson. We're just conducting a bit of routine inquiry around the area," she said. She was still trying to figure out a way to do this that wouldn't immediately put the woman's suspicions up, but it was difficult to think of one. "We just wanted to know whether you've noticed anything odd in the local area recently."

"Like that girl that ran out of the woods?" the woman asked immediately, and Tara groaned inwardly. She kept the polite smile pasted on her face, trying not to react.

"Anything at all, not just that," Tara said. "Anyone behaving suspiciously, for example. It could be a neighbor who started acting strange, or a new person in the area who raised your suspicions in some way."

"Are you trying to catch the man who made her run like that?" the woman asked, dusting off her flour-covered hands even more as if she was getting ready to write something down. "What did he do? Should we be alarmed?"

"At this stage we don't have any more information about that case, ma'am," Glenn cut in. "Like we said, we're just doing some routine inquiries. It's good to check up on the community at times like this. If there's anything at all…?"

"No, I haven't seen anything," she said, then paused to think for a moment. "Although Brenda and Jimmy up along the north shore have been fighting a lot lately. Diana thinks they're going to get a divorce. But they can't, you see because they have Brenda's grown son, Eric. And if Jimmy and Brenda divorce then, well, when she dies, he gets the lot. So Jimmy's going to fight that, mark my words, he'll fight it all the way."

Tara tried not to grimace as she nodded. "Okay, well, thank you for your time," she said. She didn't waste her breath trying to explain that a rumored divorce wasn't exactly cause to be 'suspicious.' The woman didn't know anything. If she did, she would have volunteered it right away – she seemed like the type to gossip. "We'll be heading on now."

"Alright, then," the homeowner said, but she didn't actually close the door until Tara and Glenn had walked all the way back to their car and got in.

"How do you feel that went?" Glenn asked, glancing at Tara in the passenger seat as he started the engine.

Tara cleared her throat, looking out of the window. "Not wonderful."

"What do you think our chances are of this not spreading across the whole lake before we even get to the next house?"

Tara scowled at him. "Well, you could have taken the lead!" she exclaimed.

Glenn chuckled. "No, no. I'm all for empowerment of women in the workforce. You're senior to me; I'm not just going to barge in and steal your thunder."

"So kind," Tara replied sarcastically. She breathed out heavily as they rounded the corner toward the next turnoff, the next property for them to check out. "We never had any chance of keeping this under wraps, did we? Not if the town has already been gossiping about the runner."

"Nope," Glenn replied cheerfully. "And with the amount of ground we have to cover between just the two of us, it's pretty likely that the attempted murderer is going to be out of his property and on the run before we even get to him. Unless he's a total loner and doesn't participate in community gossip, of course."

"Of course," Tara muttered. "Well, let's hope for that. And let's hope he's actually staying at this lake, not one of the many other places in this local area he could actually be."

"Yeah," Glenn said more soberly. He pulled the car to a stop outside the next property. "Here's hoping. She didn't give us a whole lot to go on. Miley Piper, I mean."

"She was traumatized," Tara sighed. "I don't know. Maybe she'll remember more, the more distance she gets from it. But right now, she's still terrified. I wouldn't be surprised if we never get any more details than that. But at least if we do get someone in as a suspect, we can do a voice lineup and ask her to identify him."

"Let's keep going," Glenn said, getting out of the car. "Someone must have seen something."

He walked over and knocked first this time, on a door that matched the previous one except that it was painted blue. Some of the lakefront properties had been built by the same developer, and it showed: cookie cutter little cabins which lured in retirees and out of towners to their vacation homes.

The door opened to a man in casual, soft-looking clothing, all in tones of brown and blue. He was gray-haired but in a steely tone that told of dark hair just turning. "Hello," he said, with absolutely no surprise at all.

That wasn't a good sign.

"Hello, sir," Glenn started. "I'm Deputy Grayson, and this is Deputy Sheriff Strong. We're just checking in on people in the local area and seeing whether you've noticed anything unusual or suspicious lately."

The man folded his arms, leaning against the doorframe. "Is there someone out there abducting girls?" he asked. "That's what Mrs. Pincher said."

"Mrs. Pincher?" Tara asked with a raised eyebrow.

The man nodded back in the direction they had just come from. "She says you're looking for someone who attacked that girl last night. So, what is it? Abduction, or something worse? Do you think he only goes for young girls, or are we all at risk?"

"Sir, we can't talk about ongoing cases at this time," Tara said firmly. Inside, she was screaming. It had already started. They had talked to one person, and it had already started. "We'd just like to stick to the questions, if we can."

"Oh, well," he leaned in conspiratorially. "I heard that Frank over on the east side has a thing for young girls. You know Frank? He has lived there on his own since his wife left him. He had an affair with this twenty-something."

Tara resisted the urge to grind her teeth – just. Someone having an affair with a younger woman was a very far cry from abduction and attempted murder. And it sounded like it was only a rumor, anyway. That was the kind of thing they were going to keep coming up against now that the rumor mill was in full session.

"Do you recall anything different, specifically in the last week or so?" she asked instead. "A new person hanging around, or something strange that you wouldn't normally see?"

The man looked to the side, thinking. He thought hard. Tara began to see that it was fairly obvious he was just trying to think of something, anything, so that he could remain part of the story. "There was a lot of hubbub last night," he said.

"Yes, we're already aware of that," Glenn said quickly. "Alright, thank you for your time. And if you do see anything suspicious, remember you can always call the Sheriff's department to let us know."

"Oh, yes, of course," he replied, looking a bit put out that they were leaving and clearly hadn't decided to take his lead seriously.

Tara pointedly set off towards the car and their next property, not wanting to waste any more time on someone who had nothing to tell them.

Glenn followed her after a second – probably a second in which he had given the man a polite nod or gesture. He was doing a lot better with this case than Tara was, she reflected. She felt such an urgency that all these delays were grinding on her soul, but he had managed to retain his big smile and polite manner. He was probably better suited for being a deputy in this kind of small-town county than she was.

She'd always wanted more. She had even considered moving to a larger place, where the Sheriff's department looked after a city or a place with a lot more problems, but she hadn't wanted to leave her family. Things like this didn't happen here in Edgar County.

Except that now, they had.

Tara knocked on the next identical door, this one painted sage green. It opened after a long moment in which she had almost been about to reach up and knock again. A woman in yoga gear stood there with her hair up in a ponytail; she was closer to Tara's own age, perhaps her late twenties, and her fit and toned body was exceedingly evident through the tight fabric. Tara slid her eyes sideways to catch

Glenn looking at her open-mouthed for a second before he caught himself.

"Ma'am, we're from the Sheriff's department," Tara said, already getting tired of the same old spiel every time – and lord knew how many hundreds of these conversations they still had yet to have before they were done. "We're trying to see if anyone in the local area has noticed anything unusual or suspicious recently."

"Well, there was that man in the pickup truck," she said immediately.

Tara raised her eyebrows, glancing at Glenn with interest. "What man?" she asked.

"He was driving around near the lake and lurking," she said, giving a light shiver. "He kept parking and just watching me. I was practicing yoga out here in the fresh air and he really creeped me out. I ended up going inside to get away from him, and I guess he drove off. He had this horrible, garish purple truck."

"When was this?" Tara asked.

"A few days ago," she said. She thought for a moment. "Thursday."

"Did you get the license plate?" Glenn asked, taking a notebook out of his pocket.

"No," the woman said, looking a little crestfallen. "I mean, I saw it, but once he drove off I just forgot about it. I didn't write it down or anything. I think they were Colorado plates."

"Alright, well, that's great anyway," Tara said, nodding to Glenn. He nodded back. It allied with what Miley had said: a local accent and now local plates. The attacker must be from within the state, if not the county. "Thank you. If you think of something else, please do call the Sheriff's department and let us know."

"I will," she promised.

Tara turned away, taking Glenn with her as the door closed behind them. "What do you think?" she asked him quietly. She glanced around at the lake in front of them. There were no pickups there now, purple or otherwise. "It sounds like stalking behavior. Maybe scoping out his victim."

"It could be," Glenn nodded. "We have to choose, don't we? Carry on talking to locals door to door in search of more evidence, or pursue this lead."

“Hmm.” Tara thought to herself that they could skip the tedious door-knocking if they had already found the one major clue that would lead them to the attacker.

They were walking toward the car when another one drove past them – a car that Tara recognized with a drop in her gut. It slowed as it passed by them, coming to a stop so the passenger could lean out of the window and call out to them.

“Hello, Deputy Sheriff!” she called out.

“Hello, Ms. Peablossom,” Tara responded, not particularly wanting to. Lydia Peablossom was a gossip, and if talking was an Olympic sport, she would have been a gold medalist. “We can’t stop. We’re on official business.”

“It’s about that girl, isn’t it?” Lydia asked, but Tara held up a hand as if she was waving goodbye and then practically threw herself into the car to avoid her. After a moment’s pause, the car Lydia was in sped up – going in the direction of the next property they had to visit.

“Well?” Glenn asked from the seat beside her. He looked at her expectantly. He was right about her being the senior one of the two of them. It was down to her, apparently, to make this choice.

Rumors flying everywhere weren’t going to help solve the case. Solid leads were.

“We go after the pickup truck,” Tara said determinedly.

She wasn’t going to let this creep get away. Now they had a lead, she would chase it down until they found him.

She wouldn’t let him attack another girl again.

CHAPTER FIVE

Tara rubbed her fingers together for a moment, limbering up as the program loaded on the ancient computers the Sheriff's department had to work with. "You rea?" she asked Glenn.

"Nearly," he said. His tone was distracted, focusing on the screen in front of him. They had sat down at their usual desks, facing one another, computers back to back in one corner so that they could still see each other and talk easily.

"I've got mine up," Tara said, quickly typing in a query and filtering the results with a few tick boxes. She was looking for people who owned purple pickup trucks and were registered in the state, while Glenn was looking up the names of registered owners of properties on or near the water. Her list loaded and she looked at him expectantly.

"Okay, ready," he said.

It wasn't as simple as just reading the address the truck was registered to. A lot of people around here would have a home somewhere in one of the towns and then a second property by the lake. "Anthony Adams," she read out, the first alphabetical response. Thankfully, the list of purple pickups was not long – though it was longer than she might have expected for such a specific color.

"No match," Glenn said after a moment, peering in at his screen and scrolling up and down with his mouse.

"Okay," Tara said. "James Bartholemew."

"No match."

Tara sighed and took a breath, scrolling to the next name. This was going to be tedious. She started to read them out mechanically, barely paying attention to what she was saying out loud. All she heard was the constant reply: no match.

There had to be someone on this list who matched up to what they were looking for. There had to be.

"Xavier Hume," she read aloud, waiting for the inevitable response.

"Wait," Glenn said. "H-U-M-E?"

"Yes," Tara replied, catching her breath – but not letting herself get her hopes up yet.

"That's a match," Glenn exclaimed. "He owns a house on the lake just above the one we were asking around at."

"Just above?" Tara asked. "How far?"

Glenn glanced over his shoulder at a huge map of the county that was pinned across one of the walls of the station. "About a twenty minute drive."

"Then it could be him," Tara said. She clicked on the record she had for the vehicle, opening it up. "Hold on. This says he is registered as having sold the truck two months ago."

"Two months?" Glenn asked. "Isn't that mighty convenient?"

"He could have reported it sold in order to cover his tracks so he can keep using it. Look him up in the system," Tara urged. "I'm getting his home address. Looks like he's from out of town. A different county."

Glenn typed and clicked around for a moment, then paused as he waited for the results of his search to load. "He has a record."

"What?" Tara demanded, her head snapping up. A purple pickup, a lakeside property, and a criminal record? How much better of a match could this man be?

"He assaulted a woman in her early twenties a few years ago," Glenn said. Then he whistled. "There's a picture of her facial injuries submitted as evidence. She was a redhead."

Tara only just held herself back from gasping out loud like she was in some daytime cop show. "You're serious?"

"This has to make him an extremely good suspect, right?" Glenn said.

"Better than good," Tara said, switching off her screen and getting up, grabbing her cell phone from her desk. "I'd say he's suspect number one. Come on. We have to go and talk to him."

"I thought you said he was out of county?" Glenn replied.

"We'll figure that out on the way," Tara told him, heading for the door. As she did, it opened, allowing Sheriff Braddock into the station.

"Oh, Deputy Sheriff Strong!" he called out. "Any progress on your door to door interviews?"

"We have a suspect, sir," Tara said, feeling like a pony that had just been reined in. She could see the start line for the race right ahead. She wanted to go. "We're about to head off to interview him."

"Fantastic work," the Sheriff grinned. "What's the location?"

"He lives in Desmond," Tara said. "If he was here at his lakeside property over the weekend, I'd guess he's back home now that it's Monday."

"Wait a second," the Sheriff said, holding up a hand to physically stop her as she tried to walk past him. "Desmond?"

"Yes," Tara said impatiently.

"That's not in Edgar County," Braddock pointed out.

Tara sighed. "I know, but we need to go and talk to him."

"Just hold on up," Braddock said, shaking his head. "We need to be careful, here. You have to be respectful when crossing jurisdictions. Your first step is to coordinate with the department over there and get everything set out in terms of who gets to do what."

"Sir," Tara argued. "We can't rely on someone else to do this investigation. They don't know what we're dealing with. They might not ask the right questions – they might miss something. And I don't want interview notes second-hand. I want to look him in the eye and watch his reactions. We've got to be the ones to do the interview."

"You can negotiate that when you talk to the locals," Braddock said. "Be careful, Tara. I mean it."

"I will," Tara promised, which was the quickest thing she could think of to say to get him to let them out. "I'll call from the car."

"Make sure she does," Braddock called after them, no doubt aiming it at Glenn, as they disappeared through the doors of the station.

Tara didn't want to wait for Braddock to be able to hold them back any further.

"You're going to call them, right?" Glenn asked as they headed to the car and opened their doors. "I don't want him coming down on my head later. It's alright for you, the golden child."

Tara rolled her eyes as she got into the car and buckled up. "I'm not the golden child. And I don't want them getting to him first. I mean it. We have to be the ones to ask the questions."

"You still have to call them," Glenn groaned. "You heard him, didn't you? And we don't want to run into legal problems later about jurisdiction that could get the case thrown out."

"I'll call them," Tara said, looking right ahead as Glenn pulled out and began following the instructions of the GPS.

"Okay?" Glenn said expectantly, given that Tara hadn't yet moved to pick up her phone.

"I'll call them," Tara repeated. "When I'm ready."

Glenn groaned, a strained noise which suggested she was putting him in a very difficult position.

"It's going to be fine," Tara said, ignoring him. "I just don't want to give them enough notice to be able to beat us there. I'll start the call when we cross the county line. It's only a short drive from there. And we'll technically be playing it by the book, letting them know that we're coming over. I'll tell them I want to be the first to talk to him but it's okay if they come, too. And then when we get there, I'll say we had to go in right away to avoid the risk of him looking out front, seeing the car, and then running out the back."

"I hope you know what you're doing," Glenn said wearily, obviously already resigned to letting her get her way.

Privately, Tara hoped she did, too.

But she wasn't going to let self-doubt get in her way now. They knew who had attacked Miley Piper, and he wasn't going to get away with it. There was no way she was going to trust this to anyone else.

Tara was going to arrest Xavier Hume, and no jurisdictional politics were going to stop her.

CHAPTER SIX

Tara hammered on the door and then stepped back, trying not to be intimidated. The property the GPS had taken them to was at least three times the size of her parents' home – and that in itself was twice the size of her own.

"He must be in," Glenn said, nodding to the Jaguar parked in the driveway, a status symbol that clearly smacked of the amount of money the resident commanded.

"Unless he has several cars," Tara muttered.

She checked her watch. It was past ten in the morning – four hours since the start of her shift when all she had on her radar was finding Billy Westfoot. It was more than possible that Xavier Hume was somewhere else, at work.

There was a clattering noise somewhere behind the door and then it clicked open, revealing a man in a sharp suit with a thin red tie that he smoothed down as he looked at them. He was maybe in his early forties, well-groomed and smooth-shaven. "Can I help you, officers?" he asked, looking down at them from the slightly elevated position of the door.

"Xavier Hume?" Tara asked, immediately taking the measure of him. He was tall and broad shouldered. Enough to be able to grab a young woman from the street and shove her into the back of his car, for sure. Maybe not the Jaguar. Since he had the pickup truck, it was likely he'd used that.

"Yes," he said, fiddling with one of his cufflinks. "Is this important? I'm on my way to court."

Tara raised her eyebrows. "Are you up on charges?" she asked. That would explain the sharp suit.

Hume snorted a laugh. "No. I'm representing the defendant."

Oh.

He was a lawyer.

Tara's heart sank. If there was one thing lawyers knew, it was how to get out of charges. To get out of interviews. To say nothing at all.

The second she knew he was a lawyer, she knew the difficulty of this case had just been turned up to eleven.

"Perhaps we can speak for five minutes," Tara said, gesturing inside. "I'm afraid this is really rather important."

He looked them over for a second, pausing now. He turned back from the door with a kind of exasperation, gesturing inside. "I'm just packing my briefcase," he said. "You have until I'm done."

Tara gritted her teeth against the insolence of that remark, as if he was so important that solving an important case – and possibly saving lives – had to wait for him to deign to give his attention. Glenn made a tiny sketch of a bow, allowing her to step inside first, and Tara did so.

The home was just as opulent inside as the outside suggested. The marble-lined entrance led on to plush carpets, a hallway stacked with diplomas and certificates in a long row that stretched as far as the back of the house. Hume led them off to the side, through a doorway that led into an elegantly appointed sitting room with a fireplace in that same marble.

There was a briefcase on a coffee table in the center of the room, as suggested, and he went directly over to it to continue selecting and packing papers and files. "Talk, then. Your window of opportunity is closing."

Tara gritted her teeth momentarily. She hated this guy already. His attitude was so arrogant, she was glad she was going to be able to put him in handcuffs. He hadn't batted an eyelid at their arrival, but that was probably just because he was an experienced enough lawyer to have spoken with a lot of law enforcement and he knew how to keep a poker face.

"We're looking into a case which happened in the local area," Tara said. She glanced at Glenn, who had lingered near the doorway as she stepped into the room. That was smart. He might be able to head off any attempt to run. "We'd like to know where you were over the last few days."

"Few days?" he looked up at her and snorted. "You want an itemized schedule for every moment of my time?"

"Well," Tara said, squaring her shoulders. "Yes. That would be very helpful."

The lawyer shot her an annoyed look and shut his briefcase, clicking the locks into place. "You could have just called my secretary."

"If you could give us their details, we'll be happy to liaise with them on the proof of your alibis," Tara replied evenly. "But we're asking you now."

Hume swung his briefcase off the table and into his hand, clearly ready to go. "Excuse me?" he asked, his tone rising and getting harder. "You're asking me for an alibi?"

"Did I not make that clear enough?" Tara asked, knowing full well that she had. "We are investigating a crime, Mr. Hume. That means we need to rule you out from our suspect list."

"Well, you can rule me out," he said, shaking his head and brushing by her – only to find himself facing Glenn, who was doing his best attempt at making himself as wide as possible.

"Sir," he said. "I would really advise that you simply answer our questions, so we can all get on with our day."

The lawyer snorted again, then looked back at Tara over his shoulder. He had one hand in the pocket of his expensive-looking suit, the other hand holding his briefcase, and he looked absolutely unafraid. "Really?" he said. "You're going to have to subpoena those records. I'm sure that wouldn't be a problem because you've already spoken to a judge about the case, right? After all, this is outside of your jurisdiction, so you must have a lot of connections working on this and making things easy for you. Right?"

Tara faltered for a moment, opening her mouth only to find she couldn't find the words to say to justify herself.

Hume laughed. "Right. So you're here outside of your jurisdiction, without permission, without clearance, and with no leg to stand on. Get out of my way, deputy. I've got to get to court, and if you obstruct me, you're the one who is going to be up on charges, not me."

"If you could just -" Tara began, but there was a loud knock at the door which surprised all of them.

Hume gave them an exasperated look and pushed past Glenn, who offered no resistance under the circumstances, to go back to his door. Tara waited where she was, Glenn watching from the hall – and so she saw his face blanch when Hume answered the knock.

"Hello," Hume said, with some smugness. "Well, well, well, this is interesting. Now, are you here to talk to me, or to liaise with your colleagues from out of county?"

Tara swallowed.

There was a voice from outside, muffled so that she couldn't make out what it was saying, and then Glenn was backing up to allow Hume back into his own sitting room. This time he was followed by two officers dressed in the uniform of the local Sheriff's department – the same as their own, but with a different patch on the arm indicating their jurisdiction. Each of them looked Tara up and down with frowns, as if examining something that was out of place.

"What's going on here?" one of the pair, a tall man with a bald head, asked to the room in general.

"We're here to question Mr. Hume in relation to an incident in Edgar County," Tara said, steeling herself to make a stand. "I spoke to a coordinator for your county over the phone."

"I believe you were told to wait until we could arrive and speak to the suspect together," the other deputy told her sharply.

"This is a time-sensitive investigation," Tara began.

"Every investigation is time sensitive," the deputy snorted. "That's no excuse for breaking protocol."

"Talking of things being time-sensitive," Hume interrupted, his voice supercilious and carrying over all of them easily. "I really do need to get to court. I've been out of the loop for two weeks while I was overseas, so I needed to get there early – bad enough to miss that, but if I stay for the floorshow, I'm going to be late. Perhaps you could play out the whole thing and then let me know later who won the right to actually talk to me."

"Wait," Tara said, her heart pounding hard in her chest as she realized that maybe all of this was for nothing. "You were overseas for two weeks? When did you get back?"

"Late last night," Hume said. "I had a lovely vacation, and you people are ruining my vibe. Now, come on, so I can lock up."

He was making a shooing movement with his hands, and this time, Tara actually obeyed him.

"There's no point in having this argument," she sighed at the tall deputy. "He has an alibi."

If he had been in the county last night, that meant there was a chance he would have been at the cabin. But it was moot. In order to kidnap Miley Piper and take her to the cabin in the first place, he would have needed to be around the day before. If he'd been on a plane on his way back into the country, that would make it impossible for him to be the man who had abducted her. The purple truck was nowhere to be seen, which tallied with the report that it had been sold – and the new registered address had been out of state. That truck was gone. And in the end, Tara had to admit to herself that the guy their witness had seen parked by the lake shore might not be related to their killer at all. It had always been a tenuous lead to start with.

They had just built up a lot of bad will with the neighboring county, probably got into trouble with Sheriff Braddock, and messed up in front of a big hotshot lawyer – all for no reason at all, since he wasn't even the man they were looking for.

Tara's mouth went dry.

And the worst part of it all was that they had wasted time chasing down a single lead instead of getting more statements from other locals who might have actually seen the abductor – and he was still out there somewhere, roaming free.

CHAPTER SEVEN

He looked out over the lake, brooding slightly. He felt incomplete. Aching. Like there was a large hole inside of him.

He hadn't expected to feel this way – not today. Today he should have been riding high on the wave of success. There was always a kind of afterglow after a plan went well. Days or even weeks when you looked out to the horizon and felt a swell of pride and happiness at what you had managed to achieve. How you'd gotten away with it. How no one in the world even suspected you. You could walk down the street and know how much better you were than anyone you passed. You could let that superiority buoy you, even look at a Sheriff or a cop and nod and smile good morning. Because you knew that you had beaten them.

Today should have been a good day. A rise with the sun, smile at the view over the lake, nod to your neighbors, and go for a long walk in town kind of day. But instead here he was, standing on his doorstep, brooding, and looking over the lake with his arms folded over his chest.

He missed her. Her absence was like an itch he couldn't scratch. He wanted to reach for someone who wasn't there. She had been there last night and then she'd run, and she had ruined the whole plan. Sent him down into this spiral.

This wasn't how the plan was supposed to have worked out.

Over the years, so many of them had gone perfectly. Every girl was different, of course. Some of them fought to the end. Some of them went meekly into the night like they were just doing what they were told. Almost all of them thought they were going to escape right up until they didn't. They thought they could either talk him out of it or fight their way out, or else that someone was going to come and rescue them.

No one ever came to rescue them. That was one thing you could rely on, almost always. No one even looked for them until it was too late, and if they did look, they looked in the wrong place. He was careful enough about that.

He should wait for a while before the next one. He had to be patient. He needed to leave some room, make sure that there was no suspicion falling on him before he acted again. He had always tried so hard not to be overzealous. If you left some time between your girls, then no one poked around and asked questions. No one made connections. If you left time and let things settle, people would have forgotten by the time you took the next one.

He had to wait.

But there was this girl, and he'd managed to get his eye on her…

Oh, she was a good one. She would be a wonderful way to make up for the disappointment. He missed her – the other one – so badly. He'd had a whole plan in his mind for how it would all work out, and now she was gone. It would be nice to take another.

He would have to wait. Maybe not as long as he usually did. Maybe just for a while. He would have to restrain himself.

Oh, but she was lovely. And no one would link the two cases, would they? Or even if they did – he didn't think she would tell them enough, the one who was gone, to find him. He couldn't believe she would do that. There were things she didn't know. No one would find him just because he took one more lovely girl for his collection. He had everything ready for her, didn't he? There was no sense in waiting, not really. And how beautiful she would be. How scared. How she would tremble when he put his hand on her back, leaving the blindfold on so she could not see how close he was or what he was holding.

No, no, no. He was going too far. Allowing himself to think about her so much. That would only increase the pull to take her, and if he did that, he would increase the risk of being caught. But…

Wouldn't he love to see her tied up in his room in the cabin, just waiting for him, just ready to be plucked like a flower planted in the soft earth?

But if he didn't wait, they would be onto him. He bit his lip, trying to stifle the desire with the pain. He promised himself that he would wait. He would wait and try not to remember how he had beaten the police every time so far, how he had always kept the upper hand.

He would wait and try not to let it all go to his head.

CHAPTER EIGHT

Tara slumped into the chair in Sheriff Braddock's office, knowing she was in for a verbal beating.

"Right," Braddock said, closing his door and moving over to stand behind his desk. He looked for a long moment at Tara, who found she had to look away, and then at Glenn beside her. "Does anyone want to explain to me this huge mess that has just landed on my desk?"

"I just wanted -" Tara started, but Braddock held up a hand.

"That was a rhetorical question," he said. "Because I know exactly what happened. I told you to take your time and liaise with the deputies in the other county, and you didn't. I told you to respect jurisdiction, and you ignored me. And you did all of this while trying to question – and I really can't believe this last part – a *criminal lawyer*."

"Sir, this was a difficult situation," Glenn began. "We needed to make sure we got to the suspect in time."

"I'm not even talking to you, Deputy Grayson," Braddock said, holding a hand against his head. Then he gestured towards him. "Tell me this. Was it your idea to go after him before the locals?"

"Well," Glenn began, shooting Tara a guilty look. "I think it was really a mutual decision, you know, something we both felt was…"

"So, it was Deputy Sheriff Strong's idea," Braddock said. He sighed. "Really, Grayson, your loyalty is commendable - but it's not going to get you very far. Go on, you're dismissed. Go."

Glenn opened his mouth – Tara saw him from the corner of her eye – but then Braddock pointed at the door and Glenn must have known he was done. He got up, giving Tara another of those guilty looks, and left the office.

Sheriff Braddock sighed again, walking around the desk, and sitting on the edge of it, right in front of Tara.

"Tara," he began, wearily, switching to her first name instead of her title. The change didn't go unnoticed. Tara knew he was trying to talk to her on a level to which he thought she would listen. "You know you're my second in command. My right hand. You know I'm backing you to be Sheriff when I'm gone, and that's why I let you do your own thing and take your own lead most of the time."

Tara opened her mouth to argue, but he held up a hand to cut her off.

"But I can't have you acting this way – like some rebellious teen," the Sheriff said. Tara bristled at the description. "I thought we were past this phase with you. You know how it works – when you're dealing with the law, by the book is best. If you go off script, all you're doing is opening it up so you can have the whole case thrown out by some clever lawyer who knows about loopholes – like that one you riled up this morning. And we're lucky to even get this case. Most of the time, a small department like us has maybe two or three days max before the state police take over. You might have just sped up that timeline."

"I know," Tara sighed. She knew the lecture. When she'd first joined the department, she'd had a rebellious streak – that much was true. She had bucked the rules, tried to take shortcuts in order to get cases finished quicker. She'd learned the hard way – thankfully only in small, petty cases – that doing so was a quick route to never having a conviction actually stick.

"Right now, we have a potential killer out there," Sheriff Braddock continued. "A man who tried to kill, and is likely to do so again. If we don't catch him before he does, given the opportunity to stop him now, we'll have blood on our hands."

Tara wanted to disagree – wasn't it melodramatic? – but found she couldn't. He was right. There was no other way to slice it. If she had the opportunity to stop a killer, it was her sworn duty to do so – and failing to stop him would mean she bore some of the responsibility.

"Maybe we need to look at things from a different angle," Tara said. "If we look at it from outside the box, maybe we can see something that we've missed so far."

"It's a good thought," Braddock said.

There was silence for a moment as they both thought hard. Tara twisted things over and over in her mind. How could you track someone without a description of what they looked like, where they were, or even what vehicle they drove? Without any security footage to follow?

"How do we know that he's a killer?" Braddock asked, cutting into her thoughts with the tone of someone who had just made a big mental leap.

Tara stared at him for a moment. "We have witness testimony."

"Do you believe it?"

"Yes." She looked down at her own hands for a moment, thinking. "She was terrified when I spoke to her. It's not that I don't believe her – I do really believe that she was frightened out of her mind."

"What if she was literally frightened *out of her mind*?"

"You're suggesting she may be making the whole thing up?" Tara asked, her brow furrowing. She winced at the idea. The last thing she wanted was to throw more flames on the age-old fire of victim blaming and having young women disbelieved when they spoke up about their attackers.

"Not making it up," Braddock clarified. "You seem to think that she believes it, and I trust your judgement. But what if she's wrong? What if she's not in her right mind, and she's running from something that doesn't exist?"

"So, we should just stop looking now and wait to see if anything else happens?" Tara asked. She didn't mean to challenge him, but she didn't like the way this was going.

"Just supposing that she isn't well – mentally speaking. If she made the whole thing up in her head as a delusion that she believes wholesale, or if she had some kind of benign encounter which she twisted into something darker because of her mental problems, then we could be spending a lot of time and effort looking in the wrong direction," Braddock said. "I want you to stop investigating until we get some clarity. We'll have to ask the medical professionals at the hospital to give her a proper assessment. If they don't find any evidence of issues beyond the trauma she's been through recently, then fine. If they think there's a possibility that she's delusional, then we monitor her and go from there."

"But sir – that's not…"

"Are you going to go against my direct orders if I tell you to?" His tone was bordering on confrontational, but he had taken the same pose and the same syntax that he always employed when he was teaching her something. Asking her to think for herself, to assess the situation and apply everything that he had taught her before now.

"No, of course not," Tara said quickly.

"What's your solution?" Braddock asked, bluntly. He was looking at her evenly now. He had the answer himself – he knew what he wanted her to say. She just had to find her way to it.

"We monitor her," Tara replied, forming the plan in her head as she went. "Like you said. And we'll – uh, Glenn and I will tone it down a little. But we'll keep the investigation moving. I think we really should keep going. If she's telling the truth and we lose time, then it will make things that much harder."

"Right," Braddock nodded approvingly. "There. Save resources for the most likely scenario, but keep an open mind that things might not be as you suspect. Now you're thinking like a Sheriff and not like some scatter-brained teen going off half-cocked to solve mysteries in a kid's book. Let's keep it that way from now on, yes?"

"Yes, sir," Tara nodded, bowing her head slightly. She'd taken the hit, taken the shame of making the wrong choice. Now she had to move forward and redeem herself by showing what she was able to do.

"Where are you with this truck lead?" he asked. "You struck out with the lawyer."

"There aren't any other matches to registered owners of cabins in the county," Tara sighed. "Purple pick-ups aren't all that common. I think it was either unrelated, or the witness just made it up."

"Alright. Go home," Braddock said, getting up from the front of his desk and walking to sit behind it again. "It's been a long day. We start again first thing in the morning. That is, if I don't already have a report telling me Miley Piper is mad as a hatter."

Tara nodded and left his office, not wanting to linger long enough for him to change his mind about handing down some extra discipline to be sure she got the point – or to tell her that there was to be no investigation at all.

She made her way right out of the station and got into her car. She hadn't seen Glenn on the way out, so she peered around the parking lot for his car before remembering he had probably walked to work that morning anyway. She decided to take a route through town that would align with his route home just in case she could catch up with him in person. If not, she could always text him an update.

She was moving slowly through the center of town, keeping her eyes out for a pedestrian with Glenn's telltale curly brown hair or anyone trying to drive past her. The town was quiet at this hour. Most workers would have clocked off either an hour before or would be working the graveyard shift, so Tara was able to keep her pace slow until she spotted Glenn walking up ahead.

"Hey!" she called out to him through her car window, rolling it down. He turned in surprise, saw who was calling, and grinned before walking over.

"You survived, then," he commented, leaning down to rest his elbows on the window frame.

"Just about," Tara smiled. "He made it clear I need to follow the rules from now on."

"Good," Glenn winked. "That means I don't have to be the one to keep telling you."

"I know you told me so," Tara said, sighing lightly. "But I just really thought… anyway, it doesn't matter now."

"I know," Glenn said. "You just wanted to do your job."

There was much more in the debate – about how doing the job required following the rules, and yet how the rules sometimes stopped you from adequately doing the actual job of solving crimes, and back and forth, and back and forth. But Glenn's soft smile told her that he understood the whole thing anyway, so Tara didn't bother.

"Well, I'll let you go," she said. "I just wanted to catch you before you went home, so you knew what was up. I'm heading home for dinner with my parents." A voice in the back of her head told her she should pass on the message about toning down the investigation, but she didn't want to. She believed Miley Piper. Maybe if they carried on as normal, they could tell the Sheriff they had toned it down after the fact. Pretend there might have been more to give. Lying to Braddock didn't sit well with Tara, but then neither did regarding Miley Piper as a liar or delusional without proof.

Glenn nodded and straightened up. "I'll see you bright and early in the morning," he said. "We'll reset and start again. See if we can't find ourselves another suspect."

"Alright," Tara said, and she would have driven away – but someone stepped right in front of her car, waving their hands at her.

She groaned when she recognized Lydia Peablossom, the town gossip. Whenever anything happened – no matter how small – somehow, Lydia would find a way to track you down and start asking questions about it. Apparently, their encounter near the lake had only stoked Lydia's curiosity.

“Deputy! Deputy!” Lydia exclaimed breathlessly. She was overweight and draped in a number of clashing patterns and colors of velvet fabrics, but she still managed to run across the road to catch them before Tara had time to react. “Oh, thank goodness I caught you. Is it true?”

Glenn blinked. “Is what true, Ms. Peablossom?” he asked. Tara was selfishly thankful that Glenn was the one on the outside of the car, not her – the most obvious target.

“Everyone’s talking about it,” Lydia said, giving them both a wide-eyed look. “The killer!”

“We can’t talk about active cases, Ms. Peablossom,” Glenn began, giving her the usual speech.

“Well, we deserve to know!” Lydia burst out, looking through the windshield at Tara with wide eyes. “If it’s one of us, someone within our midst, we deserve to know!”

“Is that what people are saying?” Glenn asked with interest. Rumors usually started from somewhere. Sometimes it was a random idiot who made something up, but more often, they had some kind of basis in truth. How many times had a rumor about who had a little more cash that week allowed them to track down a thief?

“Well, is it?” Lydia asked, looking between them with her wide eyes. “Is it someone from Wyatt?”

Right here in Wyatt. That was an interesting idea to explore, Tara thought. The truck had turned out to be a bust, but there was still the issue of the ‘local’ accent Miley had thought she heard.

But who among her neighbors – people she had known her whole life – had the capacity to attempt to murder a young woman like that?

CHAPTER NINE

Tara parked in the driveway and sighed, looking up ahead at the other car that had arrived before her. A very familiar car with a bumper sticker for a neighboring county's Sheriff's department.

Her sister was here.

Tara knew it was always a risk that when she came over to have dinner with her parents, Jessy Strong would be there, too. Sheriff Jessy Strong. The successful child of the family.

No, that wasn't fair. Her parents didn't treat them any differently, not really. And Jessy was a couple of years older than Tara. Given time, she was going to get there as well. She just had to keep telling herself that.

She got out of the car and walked up to the house, trying not to feel like she was a dead man walking. Going into a conversation with Jessy, though, did make her feel that way. She just hoped it wasn't going to be as tiring a night as it often was.

She didn't have to knock on the door. Her parents had lived here their whole lives, and they trusted the local community enough that they just left their doors unlocked in the evenings. They would lock up when they went to bed, but until then, anyone and everyone – family or otherwise – was welcome to just wander by for a cup of coffee and a chat.

The heat that came out of the house as soon as Tara opened the door was reassuring, a welcome balm to the cool evening air. Most of it had built up during the day in this old house, with no need for extra heating. She closed it behind her and shrugged off her jacket, hanging it up on the peg before starting to wander further in.

"Ma?" she called out, listening for a response in the direction of the kitchen. That was usually where her mother could be found – if not cooking, then reading, sewing, talking with a friend, or, in the winter, resting in front of the fire.

"In here!" her mother called back, and Tara headed right for the kitchen as she had expected.

She emerged into the room to see most of her family already sitting around the table. Her father seemed to be engaged in some kind of solemn debate with Jessy, the two of them sitting with their heads close together and serious looks on their faces as they gestured. Tara's mother was bustling over to the table with a dish laden with chicken and vegetables, ready to be served.

And then there was the empty space, the one that they always kept but never talked about. Cassie's chair. Cassie's place setting. Always laid out at every single dinner, even though she hadn't been there to sit for a decade.

Tara stepped around it to take a place at her dad's side. Sitting opposite Jessy was objectionable, but not nearly as much as sitting next to her was.

"This looks delicious, Mom," Tara said, sliding her chair neatly under the table and reaching for a pitcher in the center of the table to pour herself a glass of water.

"It's nice to have you all here for dinner," her mother said, smiling as she took her own seat at the round table, between Jessy and her husband. "It's good luck I made so much extra."

"You always make this much extra, Mary," Tara's dad grumbled. He took the pitcher next and poured himself a top-up. Apparently, Jessy had been there for long enough that she'd debated him down a whole glass already.

"Yes, well, leftovers are always a fantastic lunch," her mother replied primly. "Don't stand on ceremony, girls. Serve yourselves."

She always said the same thing, and they always waited anyway. Jessy was the first one to reach out and grab the large serving spoon on the side of the dish, allotting herself a generous portion onto her plate.

Tara reached for the mashed potatoes first and then passed them sideways to her father, grabbing a bowl of mixed peas and corn next to serve herself a spoonful. By the time the chicken came her way she was the last one to get it, but there was still more than enough for her to have a full plate. Her mother did make generous portions, that much was true. She was probably hoping that one of these days, either of her daughters might bring a man around to the table.

Or that her missing daughter might come back.

Tara took a forkful of vegetables – broccoli and cauliflower and carrots – and started to chew so she didn't have to speak. She didn't want to get into whatever debate Jessy and her dad had been having, and she didn't want to talk about her day – not without any results to give. And as always when she came back here, the wound of Cassie's absence became a new raw slash across her day, a visual reminder that she didn't have living alone in her own home.

Ten years. It should have been easier by now. It should have been the kind of thing that she didn't even think about anymore. But when there were no answers to what had happened to Cassie, the pain and the wondering never stopped. Tara was beginning to accept the weary feeling that it never would.

"How are you doing with that murder case?" Tara's mother asked. She groaned inwardly. Of course, the news would have got back to them already. Everyone else in town was talking about it, after all.

"It's early days," Tara said, hedging her bets and not looking up from her plate. "Sheriff Braddock is really down on us for playing by the book on this one. I can't say anything to anyone."

"Really?" Jessy asked archly. Tara glanced up and saw a superior look on her face, and got the distinct impression that Jessy had been waiting for an opportunity to strike. "That's funny. Considering the whole mess you got into today with that lawyer."

Tara looked at her, her mouth a flat line, trying to convey as much as possible with just her facial expression and body language that her sister really shouldn't have brought that up in front of their parents.

"Oh? What's this?" her father asked, turning to Tara. "Are you in some kind of trouble?"

"No, Dad," Tara said through gritted teeth. "We got it all straightened out."

"That was such a rookie move, Tara," Jessy scolded her. "You ought to know about jurisdictional protocol by now. Isn't Sheriff Braddock teaching you anything in that pokey little station of yours?"

Tara resisted the urge to straight-up growl into her sister's face. "It's not pokey," she retorted. "And Sheriff Braddock knows what he's doing. He even reprimanded me for it. He's -"

"You were reprimanded at work?" Mary Strong gasped, and Tara realized she'd walked right into the trap Jessy had laid out for her. By trying to defend her home station, she'd only incriminated herself further.

"It's not a big deal, Ma," Tara said, holding a hand up over her plate. "It's fine. He just told me not to do it again. And I won't. We're just dealing with a big case here and tensions are a little high."

"Oh, it's only one little kidnapping," Jessy said, waving a hand in the air. "You'll put it to rest in no time at all, I'm sure. It's not like you have a trafficking ring on your hands."

Tara gritted her teeth and held back from reacting to that one. Maybe it was a small case to Jessy, given the big city she covered and the kinds of cases they got there on a regular basis. She really had taken down a trafficking ring last year. She'd received a medal for it from the city's mayor. A medal which she had since taken to wearing on her uniform at all times. Tara was surprised she wasn't wearing it now.

But it was a big case for Edgar County – one of the biggest they had ever faced since Tara had joined the Sheriff's department, and certainly the biggest she had ever been asked to lead.

"Well, I'm sure we will," Tara said, hoping that they would be able to leave it at that.

It was a shame, really. Jessy had more experience with a wide range of different types of cases. Even killings and kidnappings. If they had a normal family relationship, Tara would have asked her for her help and opinion. Found out what kind of techniques Jessy had learned for this kind of investigation, how she might be able to cover more ground without more manpower. But instead they had to bicker back and forth like teenagers, and there was no way in hell that Tara was going to compromise her pride by asking Jessy for anything at all.

"You have to catch these kinds of things in the first forty-eight hours, you know," Jessy went on, taking a forkful of peas. "After that, the chance of catching someone goes down real quick."

"Yes, thank you," Tara sighed, stabbing a piece of chicken onto the prongs of her fork. "I've seen the many, many trashy cop shows harping on about the concept."

"Well, I'm just saying," Jessy said in a conversational tone, which was a surefire bet that she was about to say something condescending as hell. "I'm surprised you're here. Aren't you already more than twenty-four hours in? Seems like you can't be prioritizing this case if you came to family dinner."

"Sheriff Braddock told me to take off for the night," Tara retorted. "I'm going to be a lot better at investigating when I've had some solid hours of sleep – and coming here means I don't have to cook at home, so I'm saving time."

"Girls," Tara's father said slowly, a warning.

"He sent you home?" Jessy replied, tilting her head. "Huh. I thought you were his right-hand woman or whatever. I guess not."

"I'm still his right hand," Tara seethed. "He wants me to take over as Sheriff after him, and -"

"Well, not if he doesn't want you investigating the biggest case you all have ever faced," Jessy replied. "Maybe he's changed his mind about you."

Tara gritted her teeth. "You haven't got a clue what you're talking about," she said. There was no way she was going to convince Jessy otherwise. She knew from experience that Jessy was just going to carry on calmly and stubbornly, grinding away at her, trying to make her madder and madder. The best way was just to dismiss her out of hand and try to move on.

"I do have a lot more experience in these things than you," Jessy said smugly. "Both in being Sheriff, and in investigating. So you probably don't realize some things that are going over your head."

"Girls, I'm sure you're both on the right track," Mary said, trying to make some headway between them. She had stopped eating and was looking up at them both, while their father was silently shoveling food into his mouth as if he was in a completely different world. "There's no need to argue about it now."

"You're right, Ma," Jessy said, primly pushing a piece of broccoli onto her fork with her knife. "I shouldn't punch down, really. I'm sure Tara will learn all these things in the due course of time."

"Oh, yes, I'm sure," Tara snapped bitterly, having finally lost all sense of decorum. "One day I'll be as knowledgeable as the master Sheriff. I can only pray that I will learn half as much as you, the guru of all investigation. Of course, I'll have to hurry before you've single-handedly solved every case in your county and you decide to come over here and solve all of the cases in mine."

"Well, I could probably do a better job than that Braddock of yours," Jessy sniffed. "Old man from another era. He doesn't even know what he's talking about anymore. He should retire."

"So one minute he's right for not trusting me and the next minute he's senile? Make up your mind!" Tara said, throwing her knife and fork down onto the plate with a furious clatter.

"He's never been fantastic at his job, has he?" Jessy snapped back, her eyes flashing cold fire across the table now. She, too, had given up pretending to eat. "Leaving unsolved cases left and right!"

"What unsolved cases?" Tara asked, shaking her head, and wrinkling her nose. They didn't even *get* big cases most of the time. Jessy was just making things up now, saying anything she could to antagonize her.

"I can think of one pretty huge case he should have solved," Jessy shouted, throwing out a hand to point to her side.

In the direction of the empty chair at the table.

Cassie's chair.

There was a stunned silence in the room, everyone reeling from the sudden appearance of the missing Strong in the conversation. Even though the place was always set, they rarely talked about her anymore. It was just too painful. No one said her name. No one talked about the anniversaries. They were just days when quiet ruled the house, when everyone suddenly had something very pressing to do which required them to be absolutely alone.

To have her brought up forcibly into the conversation now was like having ice-cold water thrown over every single person sitting at the table with no warning.

"He tried everything he could to find her," Tara said, her voice weak, low, but still defiant.

"How would you know?" Jessy asked. "You weren't even working for him then."

"I know," Tara said. She pushed back her chair with a scrape. Cassie's absence was a raw wound and she could not, would not, accept the salt being pressed into it with the mention of Sheriff Braddock's failure. "Sorry, Mom. I'm going home."

She turned and walked out without another word. Behind her, she heard her father sigh heavily and her mother mutter something in an entreating tone to Jessy. There was no response.

Not until she was at the door, opening it to step outside, and she heard Jessy finally respond.

"It's not my fault she's so sensitive."

Braddock hadn't failed. There had been no evidence.

He couldn't have failed.

Because he was her mentor, and if he had failed to find her sister, then Tara had spent her whole adult life working for a fraud.

Tara closed her eyes for a second, slammed the door behind her, and tried very hard not to let the rage bubbling inside her turn to misery.

***

Tara looked up from her magazine and looped her headphones off her head, letting the wires tangle in front of her. The music continued to play in her MP3 player, tinny pop music audible from the discarded device.

"Are you going out?" she asked, watching her sister carefully.

Cassie turned around and grinned. "Just for a bit," she said. "You won't tell Mom and Dad, right? Or Jessy?"

Tara sat up and folded her arms over her chest. "That depends. Is that my skirt you're wearing?"

Cassie looked down at her own body, her arms wrapping across her torso as if she was nervous. "Is it okay? Does it suit me? I wasn't sure..."

"Are you meeting a boy?" Tara asked, narrowing her eyes.

"No!" Cassie exclaimed. "No, no. I'm just going out with Maddie. We're going by the lake."

"Is there a party?" Tara asked. She tilted her head. She was having fun teasing her younger sister. Cassie looked halfway between horrified of being accused of any wrongdoing, and alarmed at the possibility that Tara might insist on coming with her.

"It's just me and Maddie and maybe a couple of others," Cassie said, and her face twisted with the kind of angst only a fifteen-year-old can manage. "If they even show up. I bet they won't show up."

"Of course, they will," Tara said, coming to her rescue at last. "And miss the chance to hang out with Cassie Strong? No one would do that."

"Except, like, everyone," Cassie said, rolling her eyes. She sighed, and turned to look in the full-length mirror again. The one attached to Tara's wardrobe was the only one outside of their parents' room, so all three girls often ended up stopping by to use it. It was just a blessing that Jessy was old enough to be at college now, so there were only two of them fighting over it. "Do you think my hair looks stupid? It looks stupid, doesn't it?"

"Did you straighten it yourself?" Tara asked, grinning. She got up and stood behind Cassie, running her hands over the heat-induced sleekness of her hair. "It looks cute."

"Did I miss a chunk at the back?" Cassie asked in horror.

"You look amazing," Tara reassured her. Teasing her was only fun when she wasn't already full of anxiety and jitters. "Trust me. Amazing. And whatever boy you hope is coming is definitely going to want to kiss you tonight."

Cassie blushed. "You think so?"

"I know so," Tara told her. "You want me to drive you over to the lake?"

Cassie shook her head quickly. "I'm sneaking out," she said. "If I ask Mom she'll only say no, so I don't want to ask. If you drive me it'll draw attention to us."

"What if you sneak out and meet me by the car?" Tara suggested. "It's dark out, Cass. And it's cold. You don't want to walk all that way by yourself."

"I won't," Cassie promised her. "Maddie's going to meet me down the block."

Maddie was sixteen already, one of the older girls in their year, and her parents had given her a cute little four-by-four, perfect for driving near the lake. Tara relented. So long as Cassie was with her friend, she would be safe. Maddie was a good girl. The two of them had been the school's biggest and most notorious nerds and goody-two-shoes until this year. In fact, they still were. Sneaking out to go to the woods was probably just a desperate attempt to try to be cool which would result in the two of them ending up studying all night long anyway.

"Have fun, then," Tara said. She reached out and mussed Cassie's hair.

"Hey!" Cassie exclaimed, ducking away.

"I just did you a favor," Tara grinned. "You don't want to look too perfect, hon. Let it get messy once in a while."

Cassie rolled her eyes and scampered out of the room, heading for the back door. Tara knew the route she would take already and moved to her bedroom window, watching. She saw her sister walking through the backyard, glancing over her shoulder at the house to make sure she hadn't been seen and then waving goodbye. Tara waved back, and then Cassie was gone, into the darkness.

And then Tara followed her, like a disembodied spirit, managing to exit the house through the window and fly after her down to the lake. And Maddie didn't pick her up. And Cassie walked all the way there on her own. And a strange man pulled her into his car and tied her up in his cabin by the lake and when she woke up the next day he served her a plate full of delicious food. And when she asked him what he was doing, he told her to eat up – because right after this, he was going to kill her.

Tara sat bolt upright in bed, clutching the covers against her chest, breathing hard and ragged, biting down a scream.

Cassie had gone missing down by the lake, and now at least one girl had come close to being killed by an unknown man. A man who might well be old enough to have been around back when Cassie disappeared.

Tara grabbed her pillow and held it against her face and screamed into it – and sobbed in frustration at the fear she had imagined on Cassie's face and the fact that there were ten years between her and that moment, and no way for her to go back and comfort her baby sister.

And when she was done, she set the pillow aside with a fierce determination that no one else was going to feel that way in her county again. Not while she had the power to find and stop him.

CHAPTER TEN

Guy North had always been an early riser. He believed the old adage about worms and early birds, although in this case it wasn't the birds that were getting fed but the fish.

He leaned back in his camping chair and heard it creak, a satisfying noise that startled a bird out of the nearby trees and sent it flapping across the lake. He watched it idly. It was a lovely morning. Cold but fresh. The scent of fall was in the air, the season preparing to change. He took a deep breath of the fresh oxygen on offer, feeling like he was the first person to take it. The sun had only just risen above the far end of the lake, bathing everything in a golden glow.

There was a tug on his fishing line and he quickly reacted, reeling in whatever it was. When it sliced out of the water and swung through the air to his waiting hand, he was reasonably satisfied: a mid-sized fish, not too impressive but definitely the right size to provide the start of some good eating tonight. Three more and he would have enough for himself, his wife, and their two sons.

It was a good start.

He put the fish into an ice cooler he had brought along for the occasion, then hesitated as he looked into his pot of bait. He needed new, fresh worms. Good juicy ones that the fish would go for. He cast an eye at the soil, which was dew-covered and moist. It looked like good pickings. He grabbed a trowel out of his kit bag and went to work, beginning to turn over the soil around his chair and behind it.

He had almost enough worms when something glinted and caught his eye. Guy squinted, leaning in further. What was that…?

Something shiny – something gold, he thought.

The idea excited him and he got out of his chair, squatting beside it rather than leaning over the back. What was that glimmer? It was half-sunk in the mud, and he turned it again with the trowel, seeing the back edge of it.

Gold. Definitely gold. Maybe even something more precious – could that be a diamond under the muck? It looked like the loop of a bracelet, buried in the dirt and probably trodden down over time so that no one else had ever noticed it.

Some tourist had probably lost it here on a camping trip. Their loss was about to be his gain. He gave the bracelet a tug but it seemed to be stuck, maybe under too much mud or even a rock, so that it wouldn't come free.

That was soon taken care of. He turned the mud over again with the trowel, holding onto the bracelet as he did so, digging away until he could get it loose. There was something holding it in place, he realized something like a tree root –

He froze in horror.

That wasn't a tree root. It was white-gray and twisted and thick, but it wasn't a tree root.

It was a wrist bone.

Guy screamed and leapt backwards, dropping the bracelet, and throwing his trowel to one side, and the jerking motion pulled the rest of a skeletal hand out of the dirt as if to wave at him, mockingly.

***

The sound of the phone ringing dragged Tara out of a bleary and – thankfully, this time – dreamless sleep, her eyes popping open to the sense of urgency the noise imparted. She sat bolt upright and grabbed it, fumbling with half-asleep limbs, managing to get it to her ear before it rang out.

"Deputy Sheriff Strong," she mumbled, having seen the caller ID belonging to the Sheriff's station.

"Tara," Sheriff Braddock said urgently. "I need you down at the lake. Glenn's on the way to pick you up in the car. We've got a body."

"A body?" Tara repeated, but Braddock was rushed, too frantic to answer. The line went dead and she stared at her phone for one second.

Then the message filtered through her brain.

Glenn was on the way to pick her up – meaning, right now.

She leapt out of the bed and grabbed a clean uniform out of the closet, dressing in record time and then tying back her blonde hair to keep it out of her face rather than bothering with styling. She had time for only one quick glance in the mirror to check she was actually presentable before she heard a car horn sound outside and rushed to the window, looking out to see Glenn leaning from his car door and waving at her.

Tara grabbed her holster and strapped it onto her waist, the last thing she needed before she ran out to the car. She leapt into the passenger side and slammed the door, fastening her seatbelt as Glenn hit the gas and peeled out of the street.

"What's going on?" she asked breathlessly.

"All I know is that there's a body down by the lake, buried on the shore," Glenn said. "Guy North was fishing down there and found it."

"Jesus." Tara knew Guy North – he owned a store in the center of the town, a property he had inherited from his father. He was known to fish early in the morning to get his quiet time in before the store opened.

She tried to imagine finding a body and just – couldn't. She had only seen bodies in the morgue before, and those were bodies of people who died of natural causes or in accidents. There had been a couple of suicides in the years she had been working for the Sheriff's department, a much higher number of heart attacks – most of which didn't need Sheriff involvement – and a small number of deaths by misadventure up near the lake or in the campsites.

She'd never had to find an unexpected body in a place where it shouldn't be.

And buried – that meant murder, didn't it? Surely it had to. You didn't bury a body if the person died innocently. Not without going through the proper channels first, and she knew the area well enough to know there had never been any sanctioned burials on the shores of the lake. It was common sense. You didn't want things leeching into the waters.

"Who is it?" Tara asked. Her mouth was suddenly very dry. A body could have stayed buried in the shore near the lake for a really long time, couldn't it? Maybe even ten years.

"I don't know," Glenn said. He glanced sideways at her. "I… I don't think it's…"

"Right," Tara said, trying to swallow and coming up short. "Right, Sheriff Braddock would have said something over the phone if it was, wouldn't he?"

Unless he thought the right thing to do was to tell you in person, her traitor brain added.

Her mind raced, overanalyzing how Braddock had sounded on the phone. Was he stressed because they had a body to deal with, or because he had to tell his deputy that her sister's body had finally been found? Was he sad in general at the loss of life or specifically sad at her personal loss? Had he rushed to get off the phone because he had a lot to do or because he couldn't bear to talk to her any longer without admitting what he now knew?

Glenn reached out and squeezed her arm, taking his hand off the wheel for just a moment, and somehow it cut through all the noise in her head. Tara took a deep breath. Maybe it wasn't Cassie. Maybe it was someone else. There was still that possibility.

In the back of her head, she knew that after ten years there was a high chance that Cassie was dead. Higher than high. In fact, the number of cases in which someone had been found alive after all that time could be counted on one hand. There were bestselling books and award-winning documentaries about them because they were so rare.

But still, her heart stopped when she thought about the possibility of finding confirmation that her baby sister, forever frozen in time at age fifteen, really was gone forever. Maybe that was part of the reason why she had not investigated the case herself, even now, when she had access to the Sheriff's files and could take a look whenever she wanted.

She just couldn't bear it.

"Here we are," Glenn said, leaning forward. Tara looked up and realized that, though she had been watching through the window, she hadn't even seen the whole drive. They were pulling through trees toward the lake, on a bumpy unpaved part of the road that led right to the shore, and she could already see two other vehicles from the Sheriff's department parked as though they were flanking a white forensics tent.

A tent. She had only seen that tent a handful of times, and always for campsite accidents. Never for something like this. She had never even gone up to look inside, leaving the professionals to do their part – and the Sheriff would normally take the lead on those kinds of cases. Tara swallowed down a lump of fear in her throat and undid her seatbelt. This was her job – this was what she had signed up for. This was what she had been waiting for all this time. She wasn't going to allow this test to undo her now.

"Sheriff," she called out, heading over toward him as soon as she was out of the car. He was standing by the white tent with his hands on his hips, his head cocked downwards, clearly watching what was going on there intently. He lifted a hand in greeting but didn't turn or move, leaving Tara to rush over and see what was going on.

Glenn was right by her side as they looked down into the hole alongside their chief. A couple of white-suited forensics professionals were in there, squatting down as they carefully excavated and unearthed what turned out to be a whole skeleton. There was no flesh left to determine the gender of the body, but Tara could make a pretty good guess: there were a few wisps of awful, dry-looking long hair that had somehow survived the conditions, a half-rotted dress that covered the body where the pelvic bones didn't poke out of the holes, and a single high-heeled shoe at the other end that had survived disturbingly well.

"Do you recognize anything?" Sheriff Braddock grunted.

Tara looked at him and realized from the sharp set of his jaw that he hadn't known, until she arrived, whether it would be Cassie or not. He must have been waiting to find out with almost as much tension as she had.

"No," she said, and she was ashamed of the rush of relief that she felt. "No, I don't recognize the clothes."

There was a defined moment in which the two men on either side of her relaxed just slightly, blowing out heavy breaths as they processed the fact that they had not found their colleague's sister. Not today, at any rate. Then the tension returned as the three of them contemplated the fact that this meant they had a new dead young woman, one who was yet to be identified.

"What can you tell us, Lindsie?" Braddock called out.

Lindsie Hobbs, the county's forensics expert and coroner, glanced up and then climbed out of the shallow hole in the ground. She stepped away from it carefully and beckoned the three officials to follow her. She unhooked a white mask from her face as Sheriff Braddock beckoned over another of the deputies – Deputy Bryant – from where he was standing with Guy North.

"Right," Lindsie said, business-like as always. If she was phased by the fact that they were tackling a much bigger case than they had in the past, she didn't show it. "We have female skeletonized remains, aged somewhere between eighteen and twenty-five. The bones are still articulated, which means she was buried in a closed grave and wasn't disturbed by animal scavenging. However, it's waterlogged ground, so we're going to need to be extremely careful with the excavation – these bones are likely to be weak and damaged. She's been in the ground for a few years."

"Why did he bury her in such a shallow grave?" Glenn asked. "She's right by the surface."

"Ah – no," Lindsie said, holding up a finger. "Actually, it's much more likely that she was buried in a deeper grave. Over time, the water rises above the normal level and washes over this part of the shore, eroding the banks. Thus, the deep grave becomes a shallow grave and she rises to the surface. That's how we've been able to discover her. If it wasn't for that, she could have remained here for the rest of time and never been found."

"Can you be more accurate on the age range? With more tests? Or give us a more accurate date of burial?" Tara asked. It was going to be tough to find a mystery woman who had disappeared at some point in the last decade or so, who might have come here from anywhere in the world if she was a tourist.

"Not likely to get you any closer on age," Lindsie said, making a twisted expression. She tossed her chin-length dark hair out of her face as the slight breeze off the lake caught it. "The only things I have to go on are the fact that she has an unfused sternal end of her clavicle, which makes her likely younger than twenty-five, and the wisdom tooth that was hidden in her jaw – those usually only appear from around the age of eighteen. But even then, I could be wrong. She might be sixteen, seventeen, or even twenty-six or twenty-seven, if she was developing at a rate slightly outside the norm. As for the date range, yes, I might be able to give you more after further testing in the lab."

Tara nodded, taking the information in, trying to see how they could use the pieces of this puzzle to put it together.

"Any lead on the cause of death?" Braddock asked.

"No, not yet," Lindsie replied, glancing back down into the grave. "We'll have to see if there are any identifying marks on any of the bones. If she drowned, or was strangled manually, or beaten without her bones breaking – anything like that, it won't show up in the bone record. You may need to use your imaginations on this one."

Braddock grunted. "Imagination is the last thing you lot need to use," he said, lifting a finger in warning at his gathered deputies. "Let's rely on facts, please."

"There's one more thing," Lindsie said. She held up something in her gloved fingers – a piece of metal muddied by dirt. "It was tucked into her hand. I think it's a dog tag."

"What number does it have on it?" Tara asked. Every hair on her body was standing on end. Miley Piper had been given a dog tag, too.

"Hold on," Lindsie said. She walked to the side and grabbed a water bottle that had been left at a small table for the team to stay hydrated, took off the lid, and carefully poured water over the piece of metal as they watched. "It's a two."

Tara bit her lip. That was a match, then. She stepped closer and examined the tag in Lindsie's hand. It was the same as the one Miley had given her, except strangely much newer looking, like it had been cast and then put in the grave without being touched ever again.

"Victim number two," she said.

Victim number two – and if Miley was number five, then…

There was a hushed silence over the group for a moment.

"I'd better get back to it," Lindsie said softly, melting away to get back into her pit.

Tara nodded in the direction of Guy North, who stood with his hands shoved into his pockets, hunched over, looking out over the lake. "Has anyone interviewed the witness yet?" she asked. She would feel much better if she was doing something.

Braddock gave her a look – not quite a smile, but a gleam in his eyes that told her he approved of her taking the initiative and showing she could follow investigative protocol. "You can have that honor, Deputy Sheriff Strong," he said. "Take his statement and let him go home once you have everything."

Tara nodded smartly, then glanced at Glenn – it being understood, naturally, that her partner would go along with her.

She left the Sheriff and Deputy Bryant standing near the white tent, finding Guy North in a pocket of relative calm beside the lake. The water lapped gently at the shore, a breeze skimming along it and raising the wings of birds who picked and dove over the center of the lake for food. Her own head was spinning, her stomach churning, but she tried to find some inner calm in order to project it towards him.

"Guy," she said, injecting warmth into her voice. "You must be very shaken."

"Oh – Deputy Sheriff," he said, turning as if startled to see her there. "Sorry. Yes. Yes, it's awful, isn't it?"

Tara nodded sympathetically. "Can you tell us what happened?"

"I was just digging for worms," he said. "I was digging and I saw this shiny thing, so I thought I'd turn it up a bit more. It was a bracelet. I tried to pull it out, and – it was attached to – to -"

Tara nodded again, understanding that it was difficult for him to say the words. "Did you recognize it?" she asked. "The bracelet, I mean?"

"No," he said distantly. "No, I don't know who… Oh." He seemed to wake up slightly, realizing something, and reached into a pocket. He pulled something out that was still covered in loose earth, holding it out towards her. Tara recognized the shape. A tennis bracelet.

She took it and smiled her thanks. "We'll get this cleaned up and see if someone knows who it belongs to," she said. "That's really helpful, Guy. Thank you."

"Is she…" Guy trailed off, seeming not to be able to think of an ending to the sentence. "Do you know who…"

"No, I'm afraid not yet," Tara said. She put a hand on his shoulder. "Is there anything else you can tell us, Guy?"

"No," he said, shaking his head. "I just – I just found the hand, and then I called…"

"Alright," Tara said, sensing he was far too shaken up to answer anything else anyway. "Is there someone at home you can be with?"

"Yes," he said, stirring himself slightly. "Yes, my wife's at home."

"Then go home," Tara said gently, patting him on the back. "We'll call you if we need to ask you anything else, alright? We know where to find you."

"Yeah," he said, and then the words seemed to drop home a little more and he nodded, casting around for his car. "Right. I'll go home."

Tara watched him go, carefully making sure he was out of earshot before she turned to Glenn.

"What do you think?" he asked. His face was troubled and sober.

"I think there's one thing we can say for sure," she said. "Miley Piper wasn't delusional or making up what happened to her. She really did escape."

She took a breath, looking toward the lake.

"You think it's the same attacker," Glenn stated. "Do you think it's someone local?"

Tara nodded. She looked back at him. "I don't think – I know. There's a killer on the loose in our county," she said. "And this lake must have the key to all of it. All we need to do first is identify our victim."

CHAPTER ELEVEN

Tara sighed, rubbing her eyes with her fingers, and stared down at the tennis bracelet laying on her desk in an evidence bag.

"How do we even start?" Glenn asked. They had brought the bracelet back to be cleaned up and logged as evidence, but that was only the very first bit of work they had to do. They were going to need to identify it and see if it matched anything in their database of information, such as an item that was logged as being worn by a missing person.

"Search terms," Tara said decisively. "Start looking through the missing persons database for the term tennis bracelet. If that doesn't work, maybe because the log isn't precise enough, then we'll need to search wider just for bracelet."

"Where, though?" Glenn asked.

Tara looked back at him.

"You..." Glenn's face paled in horror. "You want me to search all of the missing persons cases in the *whole United States*?"

Tara sighed pensively. "Let's start with Wyoming, Colorado, Idaho, Montana, and Utah. If that doesn't work, we can widen the search area."

"Okay," Glenn said, though he still looked daunted. "I guess I'll get started and go state by state."

"I'm looking through our local files," Tara said. "Maybe there's something in here from before our time that we don't remember."

They searched in silence, both of them frowning at their screens. There was a lot of data to go through; women went missing frequently, and though many were ultimately found either dead or alive, there were always those cases who slipped through the nets. There were even cases where someone had confessed to their murder, meaning the case was technically closed, though the body had never been recovered.

Tara watched enough true crime shows to already have a laundry list in her head of all the different serial killers who might have passed through their area. Some of them were known for attacking people in secluded campsites, especially near lakes. Could one of them have been responsible for this? But the ones she knew about had been caught and ended up in prison, while the man that had attacked Miley Piper was alive and free. If this case was related as Tara believed, then their attacker was in fact an accomplished killer – someone who had gotten away with it for years.

And was it possible that such a man would only have struck twice?

Tara's phone rang on her desk, and she picked it up without looking away from the data, straining her eyes to find some mention of the bracelet. "Hello, Deputy Sheriff Strong speaking."

"Deputy Sheriff," the reply came. Tara recognized Lindsie's voice. "I've just done some preliminary research while I wait to get the body back into the lab properly. Looking into the fabric of the dress she was wearing and the usual decomposition rate in similar conditions, I would say she must have been in the ground there for at least five years but no more than seven."

"Five to seven years," Tara repeated out loud, meeting Glenn's eyes. "Thank you, Lindsie, that's really going to help."

"I'll let you know if I get anything more precise," Lindsie replied. She hung up the phone, going quickly back to her work.

"That's our window for the body?" Glenn asked right away, his fingers hovering over his keyboard.

Tara just nodded, clicking boxes on her screen to narrow down her own selection.

"Here!" Tara exclaimed, almost unable to believe her eyes. "I've got her!"

Glenn jumped out of his seat. "Let me see?" he asked, walking around to look at her monitor.

"Here," Tara said again. She double-clicked on the image attachment that was part of the file, bringing it full screen. "That's the bracelet, isn't it?"

The image wasn't amazing quality – it looked like it was a portion of a larger image that had been blown up, showing the bracelet worn on someone's wrist. The victim's wrist, Tara thought with a shudder. The pattern of the interlocking fittings that held the diamonds – it was a match. There were probably many other bracelets that were created in the same exact style, but the fact that this image was attached to a missing persons record couldn't be a coincidence.

"Her name was Ness Griffin," Tara read. "She went missing six years ago – not far from this date, actually. September."

"She's young," Glenn breathed. There was a picture of the young woman herself, above the one with the bracelet.

"Twenty-one when she disappeared," Tara replied. "And a redhead, too. Just like Miley Piper."

"What do the case notes say?" Glenn asked.

"Let's see…" Tara skim-read in her haste, trying to get the details as quickly as possible. "She was last seen at a house party. She was hanging out with her friends, and they saw her wearing that bracelet – the shot is one that was taken on one of their phones. Then she left to walk home because she'd been drinking and didn't want to drive – she was walking away from the lake. She went missing somewhere between leaving the party and her home."

"Six years ago," Glenn frowned. "That was right before I joined the Sheriff's department."

"Three years after I did," Tara said. "I kind of remember the case, vaguely. I was only a deputy then and I wasn't involved in it. Sheriff Braddock had me holding down the fort, so I didn't get to know all the little details. We should have shown him the bracelet after we cleaned it up – he probably would have recognized it."

"Well, we have it now anyway," Glenn said. "And look at this for a detail – one of her shoes was found, but just one."

Tara checked the reference number given by that particular line of information and scrolled down the image gallery, finding it and zooming in. A high-heeled shoe. She recognized it, too. It was a match for the one that had been inside the grave, still intact.

"It's definitely her," she said. "I'll send this file along to Lindsie and get her to run DNA analysis, but it has to be her, doesn't it?"

Glenn nodded. "Ness Griffin," he said, as if committing the name to memory. "Six years ago."

Six years. It was a point that bore repeating. Tara thought about the gap. One murder, six years, and then one failed abduction. It couldn't be, could it?

"Most killers," she said slowly, "don't wait a whole six years before they kill again. Especially not those who got away with it so well that the body wasn't ever found."

"You think there's more," Glenn said, looking at her with wide eyes. He didn't look as if he disbelieved her. In fact, he looked as though he was glad she agreed with him, because he didn't want to be the only one with that thought.

"These other missing women," Tara said, looking back at her screen, remembering the list she had been going through before they narrowed it down more. Women who went missing ten years ago, women who went missing last year. It was a common enough occurrence in the mountains and lakes. People went hiking, or had camping accidents, or went into the lake in the dead of night. Most of the time you had to accept there wasn't much chance of finding their remains – they would be lost in the water or black bears, coyotes, or mountain lions would carry their bones back to their lairs.

But most of the time, you didn't assume a serial killer. You assumed an accident. People went camping and got drunk, or took trails they weren't familiar with and ended up deep in the kind of landscape where predatory animals had the upper hand. Or got lost. You heard hoofbeats and you thought about horses.

But a serial killer targeting the lake area?

That was a zebra, and Tara didn't know how they were going to catch a zebra. But she knew the first step. To examine those hoof prints in more detail and find out exactly how many bodies they might be dealing with.

CHAPTER TWELVE

Tara looked up as Sherriff Braddock held up a hand and called them to order.

Everyone who could be spared was there. Tara and Glenn, Lindsie and her forensics team called in from other counties, Deputy Bryant, the other six deputies that worked for the county, and another group of around ten who had been brought in from neighboring counties after Sheriff Braddock's call for help. Only a handful of the reinforcements had been left at the lake, guarding the scene.

"Alright, everyone," Sheriff Braddock said, dropping his hand. "Thank you for your patience. I'm going to keep this briefing quick because we've got a lot to do."

Tara glanced around again in the silence. Everyone was looking at the Sheriff with solemn faces. He'd requested that the reinforcements be deputies who had a little experience working on murder cases already, and Tara was glad to see that they didn't look any more confident or any less grim.

"As you know, we've discovered a body buried in shallow ground beside the lake," he said. "Together with our escaped victim, a survivor, we have reason to believe this case may be bigger than it looks. As a result, we're about to tackle the biggest search this lake has ever seen in recent history. We're going to be using local contractors to dig around the lake shore in search of further bodies. We also have three K-9 units coming in from the state PD. Now, these are trained cadaver dogs. We're hoping they will expedite the search by leading us right to anything suspicious."

"How long will that take?" Tara asked, speaking up. She knew, as Deputy Sheriff, that Braddock wouldn't mind her asking questions.

"We could very well be here for days, if not weeks," Braddock responded. "Those of you who are from neighboring counties may not be aware of the scale we're working with here, so please allow me to draw your attention to the map on the wall here. This is a map of our county; as you can see, the lake is a significant area to cover, and above that we have the smaller lake systems as well as the wooded area and the foot of the mountains. This is not going to be a small task. Your cooperation is going to be essential."

There was a general stirring in the room, no doubt as people took in and understood the real scale of what they were faced with.

"Now, assignments," Sheriff Braddock continued. He started to point to various areas of the room. "Everyone on this side, I'd like you to accompany each team of diggers or K-9 units and be there on the ground. Your task is to make sure everything is performed correctly, to keep the public back, and to be ready to move on any discovery. On this side of the room, you are going to be our interview team. I want you talking to every single resident along the lake, every campsite employee, every business owner. We need to know if anyone has ever noticed suspicious activity by the lake, focusing particularly on the spot where we now know Ness Griffin was buried."

Tara was included in the sweep of his arm that included the interviews. She felt disappointed, but… whatever the Sheriff thought was best, she would do.

"Three exceptions," the Sheriff said, holding up three fingers before everyone could start to move and talk. "Deputy Sheriff Strong and Deputy Grayson, I want the two of you here. We need you working through our missing persons cases from the park, the lake, and the mountains – anyone who went missing within our borders. We need to build up an understanding of who we're looking for in case we do find another body. I want you to become experts on those cases, got it?"

"Got it," Tara nodded smartly.

"Deputy Bryant," Sheriff Braddock said, his head wobbling a moment as he looked around the room before finding and focusing on the other man. "You're on phone duty. I want you by your desk at all times, ready to intercept any tips we get from the public."

"Yes, sir," Bryant agreed.

"We have to be fast and accurate here," Braddock said. "Not just to save lives – though we do want to save lives. But if we're not fast about it, we're going to lose this case to the state police. I don't want that to happen. I think we're more than capable. So, let's solve this case."

There was a general murmur of agreement in the room.

"Alright, that's it," Braddock said, lifting his hands in the air as if raising a barrier that was holding everyone back. "Off you go!"

Tara stayed put as the other deputies around her began to get up and rush around. For a long moment she felt like she was perched on a stone in the middle of a fast-moving river, trying desperately not to get swept away. But the room emptied within minutes, leaving just her and Glenn behind once it was done.

"No pressure," Glenn joked, breaking the silence.

Tara gave him a crooked half-smile. "None at all," she said. "We just have to identify every single victim who could possibly be up there. No big deal."

Glenn chuckled. He got up from his chair and extended a hand towards her with a sketched bow. "Are you ready, my lady?"

Tara smirked. "You're weird when you're nervous," she said, taking his hand anyway and letting him help her up.

"Yeah, well, I have a very good reason to be," Glenn said. "Nervous, I mean. Not weird. Although, working with you…"

"Alright, alright," Tara said, leading the way out of the breakroom they had used as the only spot big enough for the briefing and back toward their desks. "Enough playing around. We'd better knuckle down. You take anything less than three years old. I'll start three years ago from this date and work my way back."

"Got it," Glenn said. "We should compile some high-risk candidates, right? Girls with red hair and things like that?"

"Absolutely," Tara replied. "But right now, we can't rule anyone out. We have two redheads. That doesn't make a pattern. If we get three or four, then we can talk. Until then, we should include anyone who fits the right profile. Actually, just about anyone. We don't even know that he only targets women."

"Alright," Glenn sighed, as they took their seats. He flexed his fingers. "This is going to be a lot of typing, isn't it?"

"A lot of reading," Tara said. "Let's just knuckle down."

From that moment, she immersed herself in a world of tragedy – of sad stories that were destined to have sadder endings. She knew what it was like firsthand to wonder where a loved one was for years. To not know. To have no body, no proof that they were gone. That was the hardest part. When someone died, and you had a body, you could say goodbye to them. You could grieve and move on. But not knowing for sure where they were, what had happened…

Part of you kept alive that hope, that they were still out there somewhere. Kept it alive for years. Over time, it faded. One day, you weren't sure when it happened, but you thought of them and realized you were thinking of them as dead. And then you felt like you were betraying them by not hoping anymore. That was how it went. And still, after a decade, Tara always had that question at the back of her mind.

What had happened to her sweet, silly, smart sister?

She printed page after page of case summaries, grabbing a highlighter pen and marking everything that seemed concurrent with their existing cases as well as everything that was notable about each case, using different colors to make different points.

In each case file, there were pictures. Reproductions of photographs. The real thing would be down in their evidence room, filed away in the huge storage of box files which comprised every case the Sheriff's department had ever worked on. Physical things like photographs would be preserved down there even after the initial reports had been scanned in and typed up. That was the way they did things. There were so few cases here and so much downtime, it had never been a problem to keep on top of digitizing the archives. Glenn, Tara, and the other deputies had all done their part in getting old cases onto the system, making it one of the most up to date in the state.

She'd known it was the kind of thing that could make it easier to investigate in the future. But she had never imagined that they would be using it so directly in a case that was so important.

Each of the faces of the victims became ingrained in her mind. She tried comparing them against one another, trying to find common features, things that might mark them out as choices for their killer. Victims. Trying to make some kind of match to Miley and Ness, something they all possessed that had marked them out for death. So few of them had red hair.

They were all so young, the ones that stood out the most as potential candidates. Some of them only as old as Tara had been when Cassie went missing. Some only as old as Cassie had been.

Some of them were clear dead ends: cases where a teenager had been reported as saying they were going to steal a boat when they were drunk, and the next morning a boat being found in the middle of the lake with their clothes in it. Though the lake had been searched and no body found, it didn't mean it wasn't there. The bottom was silty; someone could slip underneath the silt in a disturbed region, or drift off to another part of the lake with the tide, or get caught in the propellors of another craft when they drifted up to the surface without anyone really noticing.

Others were solved and closed. Young women who had just run off with their boyfriends – or to get away from their boyfriends. Bodies that were found after a few days of searching, trapped in some mountain ravine, apparently having slipped and fallen and not been able to get back out. Even more were presumed solved because of little clues that had been found, like a scrap of a raincoat worn by a hiker turning up in the lair of a mountain lion when it was checked by searchers. Or because the person in question had gone missing during the worst lightning storm in the county's history, or during the coldest winter snap.

But even taking out these outliers, cases remained. Young women – and men, too – who had simply disappeared one day and never come back. There were always theories, usually noted by the deputies who had investigated the case. But when there was no evidence of any kind to go on, a theory could only ever remain just that.

Tara rubbed her eyes and looked at the clock on her screen. Hours had passed, taking them into late morning, and she was still wading back in time, further and further into the past. There were more cases in the recent past, a higher volume – but over time, those further back had more clues, more chance of having been solved. That meant that her cases were far more likely to be victims than Glenn's.

Even so, it was almost impossible to differentiate between them. Tara looked at her row of profiles, each of them printed and then stuck up on the wall behind her in a blank space. She looked at Glenn's, behind him. How could they even begin to sort through all of these missing people to find out the ones they needed to be investigating the closest?

The phone on her desk rang and she lunged to pick it up, hyper-aware of the kind of news that could be waiting on the other end of the line.

"Hello, Deputy Sheriff Strong," she said breathlessly.

"Tara," Sheriff Braddock replied. His voice sounded tired, strained. "How are you coming along with those missing persons? You got a good handle on them?"

Tara glanced again at the wall behind her. "We're getting there."

"Good," Braddock said, taking a deep breath. "Because we've got another body, and I'm going to need your help in identifying it as soon as possible."

CHAPTER THIRTEEN

Tara got out of the car as soon as it came to a stop and ran toward the group standing by the lake shore, all of them clustered together in a pattern that obviously pointed toward something on the ground. She hadn't even bothered to close the car door – this was more important. She needed to see.

"Sheriff!" she called out, getting his attention as she approached so that he would stand aside and let her in. She rushed breathlessly to the side of the hole in the ground that everyone was looking down into. The digger was parked, its basket hanging down like a harbinger pointing at the spot.

Down in the hole, significantly deeper than the one they had found a good ten-minute walk from here that morning, were Lindsie and one of her helpers. They had smaller hand-tools used for digging, and they were applying them to peel away layers of moist earth from what was very obviously a body.

She was a young woman, that much was again clear. Her clothing was more intact than that of Ness Griffin. She was dressed in a pink skirt and matching top, covered by the remnants of what looked like a leather jacket. Despite the mud and the decay and the rest of it, Tara recognized the get-up instantly, and her stomach dropped.

"What is it?" Sheriff Braddock asked, concern washing over his face.

Tara shook her head. For just a moment, she'd had a flash of what it would have been like to find her sister. That feeling of looking down at a body and recognizing what it was wearing. The feeling made her want to be sick. She was selfishly grateful that she knew the outfit only from the fact she had seen a picture of it not long before, and not for any other reason.

"It's one of our missing girls," she said, clenching her fists to try to keep her stomach under control. "I recognize her. I can call Glenn and ask him to double-check that I have it right in my head, but I think this is Ariyah Hopson."

"Okay," Sheriff Braddock said, which seemed to be about the level of response anyone could muster. "How long?"

"I think it was about two years ago she was reported missing," Tara said. She recited everything in her mind, closing her eyes for a moment to visualize the case file. She didn't need to try too hard. She'd been involved in the initial investigation, and she remembered taking the notes in the first place. At the time, she'd assumed just like everyone else that it was yet another stupid college student who had probably walked into the lake or right into a bear cave. "She was camping with friends and decided to go for an early-morning walk by the lake, before everyone else woke up. She left them a note and then never came back."

"Let's get back to the station," Sheriff Braddock said hurriedly. He called out to the other deputies standing around. "You stay here, guard the scene. Don't let anyone close, especially the press. We'll need a tarp up above the grave to cover it from the elements and any helicopters that decide to get an aerial shot. We're going to look at the files and get more information about our killer. This is three now. We are dealing with a serial killer, people. Let's take this seriously."

The warning wasn't even necessary. Tara saw the looks on their faces as she turned to walk back to the car. Most of them looked sick.

This was a serious investigation, and Tara knew with certainty that chilled her to her bones that her expert knowledge of the missing persons files had not been tested for the last time.

***

Tara pointed to Ariyah Hopson's image on the wall. "There she is," she said, a sinking feeling settling into her gut. She had known she was right – and even if she hadn't been, the dead young woman had to be someone. Still, seeing it confirmed as a case she had worked on herself was somehow even more devastating.

"Right," Sheriff Braddock said decisively. He grabbed the photograph that Tara had printed and then carried over to the investigation board that had gone up at the back of the room, already adorned with two pictures of the other girls. He stuck Ariyah Hopson up in between them.

"Six years ago, Ness Griffin," he said, tapping her picture. "Two years ago, Ariyah Hopson. And this year, Miley Piper. What are we seeing?"

"All young women," Glenn offered. He looked slightly sick, too, at the fact that they were now officially dealing with at least an attempted serial killer, an almost certain to be confirmed statistic before the day was up. All it took was three. "They're around their early twenties, all slim and pretty."

"So, he has a type," the Sheriff nodded. "We can start building a profile with this. Let's note it down."

He grabbed a marker from beside the board and started writing in rough capital letters below the pictures:

- SLIM BUILD
- CONVENTIONALLY ATTRACTIVE
- AGE RANGE LATE TEENS TO MID TWENTIES

"It's something, but it's not exactly specific enough to be able to narrow down our missing persons list much more," Glenn sighed. "It's a shame she's not a redhead; I thought we had a pattern going for a moment there."

"Wait a minute," Tara said. She leaned in closer to the photographs, but the printer they had at the station wasn't good enough to give her the clarity she needed. She rushed back to her computer and started going through the files, bringing up photograph after photograph until she confirmed what she knew. "There is a pattern, but it's not the hair."

"What?" Glenn asked, peering at the pictures on the investigation board as if he could figure out what she was referring to.

"Green eyes," Tara said triumphantly. "All of them have green eyes."

That added factor made something in her chest swell and drop. Like both of her sisters, Cassie had blue eyes. She was safe.

Which was a ridiculous thing to think because Cassie wasn't safe. Not at all. She was dead. And if she wasn't dead, then something even worse would have happened to her.

Tara struggled to bite back the nausea and swirling chaos in her mind, focusing on the case. All she could do was keep going forward and hope that at some point she would stop seeing Cassie everywhere.

"What else can we see about these victims?" Sheriff Braddock asked, holding his hand to his chin as he thought. "Where do they come from?"

"Ness Griffin and Ariyah Hopson are both tourists who came to stay at the campsites," Tara said. "Miley Piper was a local. I don't think we can say that he's specifically preying on women from any walk of life, just that he needs them to be in his area. His catchment zone, as it were."

"Do we know what happened to them before they died yet?" Glenn asked. "Forensically, I mean – how they died or if they were held in a cabin like Miley was?"

"We don't have full reports back from Lindsie," Sheriff Braddock grunted. "She's a little busy. She'll get us something helpful if and when she can. I don't think we can rule out the idea of him keeping them for a while before killing them. Actually, it would help him to evade our searches. He could wait for us to search an area of the lake and then dump the body after we'd moved on. That would explain how he's managed to get away with it all this time."

"It doesn't bear thinking about," Tara shuddered. All those girls, all of them so scared… and how many exactly would they find?

"No, it doesn't," Braddock said brusquely, which Tara recognized as a sign that he was trying to stay professional and keep his personal feelings out of it – for the good of the job. "What else can we say for sure about our victims?"

"They're all white," Glenn pointed out. "I think that means we can rule out any of our missing persons who come from different racial backgrounds."

"You're right," Tara nodded. "Killers rarely cross race lines, right, Sheriff?"

Sheriff Braddock nodded approvingly at the use of her training – knowledge which had been theory only until now. "We can use that and the age thing to narrow down our missing persons list significantly. Then we draw extra attention to anyone with green eyes. I want you two to have any green-eyed disappearances from the last ten years memorized to the point you'd recognize a shoelace, you got that? We need to be on this and able to identify any new victims as quickly as possible."

"But how does this help us catch him?" Glenn asked. He hesitated a moment, as if suddenly realizing he had openly challenge the Sheriff, but then pushed on. "It's great having a better idea of who his victims might be, but we still don't know who *he* is."

"More victims, more data," the Sheriff said. "Maybe we'll find something that will point his way. It's not going to be quick and easy to get the families over here for interviews, but we can work on that. In the meantime, you two can also use what you know to try to put things together. Maybe there's a guy out there who lives by the lake and whose green-eyed pretty mom was killed when she was young, and he's recreating that, or something. There's always some kind of lead. We start with what we know and we narrow it down whenever we learn something new. We need to figure this thing out with the dog tags, too."

"I'm pretty sure they relate to the number of victims he's taken," Tara said. "That would make Miley the fifth."

"Yes, but -" Sheriff Braddock stopped, rubbing a hand over his face. "I'm tired. I forgot to fill you in. Right after you left, we found the dog tag in Ariyah Hopson's grave. It was numbered with a seven."

"Seven?" Tara repeated with alarm. "But that doesn't fit." She envisioned the number in her head. There wasn't even any way you could misinterpret it – any way it could actually be a three. Or could it be a four that had partially worn off?

"Exactly." Sheriff Braddock sighed. "We'll figure out what it means later. Maybe it's a code, or maybe he has them numbered in a strange order, or maybe he just gave her the wrong dog tag. I don't know. Or maybe it was a four really. That's something we can figure out when we actually have the guy in custody – something to ask him later."

"And for now?" Tara asked.

"For now, look into men who have lakeside cabins and a history of violence towards women," the Sheriff said. He paused, looking both Glenn and Tara in the eye. "Remember one thing. The man who did this lives among us. He knows the lake, knows where he can bury a body without it being found. He speaks like us. He is one of us. He could be your friend, your mailman, the clerk at your favorite store. No one is off limits. Until we find him – he could be anyone and anywhere."

Tara felt those words settle into her soul with a chill.

Anyone and anywhere – but one of us.

Someone she knew was a killer, and she had missed it for at least six years. Well, she wasn't going to miss it anymore.

"Let's go," she nodded to Glenn, not willing to wait a single second to get started.

CHAPTER FOURTEEN

"We have to consider everyone," Tara said. "Remember?"

"Yeah, but..." Glenn made a face. "It wouldn't be one of our deputies. It couldn't be."

"Plenty of law enforcement officers have turned out to be killers before," Tara pointed out. "I mean – the Golden State Killer?"

"But we know these guys," Glenn said, shaking his head. "We would have known if something was up with any of them."

"Ted Bundy's friends didn't think he was a serial killer, even when the media released the fact that the killer they were searching for was called Ted and drove the same car as he did," Tara countered. "It could be any of us. It could be the Sheriff. It could be you."

"Fine, it could be me," Glenn said, throwing his hands up. "But it's not Deputy Collins."

"He has access to his brother's property," Tara said. She paused for a moment. "You know, that's one thing we haven't considered. Access. What if it's not someone that owns a property, but someone who has access to one, like Collins does?"

"You mean like a family member's cabin?" Glenn asked. He tilted his head. "How would we even go about figuring that out?"

Tara tapped her head. "Local knowledge. It's all in here, isn't it? Between us, we've been involved in a lot of cases over the past nine years. I was a local even before that. If someone has a record, we're likely to know it."

"That's not very precise," Glenn grumbled. "We might miss something. There must be some way to cross-search the records of property ownership against criminal records – searching for family name or something."

"If you have the skills to put that search algorithm together then you do it," Tara suggested, not meaning to sound testy but all too aware that they hadn't made much progress yet. "In the meantime, this is the best tool we've got. We have this advantage, we should use it."

"Alright," Glenn shrugged. "What do we do, just read through the names on the property deeds?"

"Yes," Tara said. She pulled up the website that she needed to search the records; thankfully, she'd already been searching local property records so much that she had a saved set of parameters that would narrow them down to lakeside cabins. "You go from the top and I'll go from the bottom. Eventually one of us should see something, hopefully."

"Wait," Glenn said, his head jerking up as if seized by a sudden inspiration. "You said something about brothers."

"Right?" Tara asked, her fingers hovering above her keyboard, ready to get on with the search if his thought had come to nothing.

"Well," Glenn said. He was frowning, furrows between his brows indicating that he was deeply thinking it through. "I just… I'm sure I remember that Donny Weston has a hunting cabin near the lake. I think he invited me over there once when we were drinking."

"You drink with Donny Weston?" Tara asked, raising an eyebrow. There was nothing wrong with Donny, per se. But his family…

"No, we were just in the same bar," Glenn said, waving a hand. "He was drunk, and thought everyone was his best friend. But anyway – when you said brother, it made me think. What about Tim Weston?"

Tara considered that in her head, summing up what she knew about Tim Weston. He was tall, well-built even if slim, so she couldn't see him having any physical problems with abducting young women. He would probably have enough upper-body strength to grab someone and shove them into a car. He was also pretty well-known for his views, which weren't exactly modern.

"How many times have we had to speak to him?" Tara asked.

"About half a dozen, at least." Glenn ticked off a few pointers on his fingers, doing mental calculations. "Maybe more. And last I heard, he got kicked out of his girlfriend's house for cheating around. He's been living there."

Tara bit her lip, thinking it over. It could be anyone they knew – that was what Sheriff Braddock had said. And Tim Weston was not a good man. He had attracted cautions over and over again for harassing and following women, not taking no for an answer, and spouting loudly about how he felt that all women should expect to be treated as property. That was the gist of it, anyway. He was one of the men in town that women who lived here knew to avoid, which of course had only made him angrier.

"We need to talk to him," she said decisively. "It's too much of a coincidence to overlook. Like Sheriff Braddock said, everyone is suspicious and we need to consider any suspect, no matter how well we know them. And I don't think anyone would be surprised that knows Tim."

"Right," Glenn said. He got up, grabbing the radio off his shoulder. "I'll let the Sheriff know. Let's get to the car."

Tara listened to him reporting their movements via the codes of their office, wincing when he said the name out loud – Tim Weston. She would have preferred to keep it under wraps for now. It wasn't that she thought that some of the deputies could be killers, but that didn't mean she thought they were good at keeping secrets. And anyone with a scanner might be listening in, which meant that members of the public could now be aware of their suspicions. She didn't say anything – what was done was done. They would just have to mitigate the damage if anything came up.

Tara rushed out to the car with Glenn in tow, jumping into the passenger seat as per their usual setup. She could easily have driven instead, but since Glenn was the junior of the two of them – though not by much – the idea was that she would be the one able to jump right out of the car and leave it running if needed.

Glenn started the car and backed out of the parking lot by the Sheriff's station, which only held space for a handful of cars. They were on the road quickly, Tara glancing out of the windows and then refocusing on the task at hand.

"We need to bring him in," she said. "Tim Weston isn't friendly to our department. If we try to talk to him in his cabin, we're not going to get anywhere. We need to put the pressure on and show him we're serious."

"It won't be easy to bring him in, either," Glenn warned.

Tara glanced at him sideways and smirked. "You're not up to it?"

"No, I'm up to it," Glenn said defensively. "I just thought you – Oh." He caught her eye and realized she was only ribbing him, and stopped.

"No, do go on," Tara said. "You thought I…?"

Glenn's cheeks darkened slightly. "It doesn't matter," he muttered.

"I'd really love to hear your thoughts," Tara said. "We have to do a risk assessment, after all. What are you afraid of, Deputy Grayson?"

Glenn rolled his eyes. "I *thought* you might want to take more precautions given that he's probably stronger than you, but that's fine. I was clearly wrong."

Tara grinned. So long as he remembered that he wasn't supposed to give her any special treatment or protection just because she was a woman, that was indeed fine.

"He may be armed," Glenn said after a moment. His tone was more serious again. "He's a hunter, and I know he does a lot of hunting from the base of the cabin. He probably has at least one gun there if not several, plus plenty of ammunition."

"We'll keep that under advisory," Tara nodded. "If he's alone and he doesn't know we're coming, chances are he won't have a chance to grab them anyway. We'll just go right up to the door and knock. No need to assume that things are going to turn bad – going in aggressive could be a self-fulfilling prophecy."

"Right," Glenn nodded. He glanced at her sideways and his hands tightened slightly on the steering wheel, but he didn't say anything else.

They stopped at a red light in the center of town – bad luck, given there were only three lights in total – and Tara stewed at the delay. Even more so when Lydia Peablossom appeared like a bad penny to tap on the window where they were stopped.

Tara rolled down the window quickly, unable to contain her annoyance. "Ms. Peablossom, please don't walk out into the road like this," she said. "You have to stay on the sidewalk. If we were to set off suddenly, you'd get your feet run over or maybe worse."

"It can't be true," Lydia said, instead of actually listening for even a second. "It just can't be one of us."

"Ma'am," Tara began, impatiently. The lights above them flicked to green, but Glenn looked over nervously and didn't move the car. She understood why. She'd only just verbally warned Lydia of what could possibly happen if he did.

"No, you've got it wrong," Lydia said. "Everyone agrees. Tim Weston wouldn't hurt anyone like that. Not that bad."

"Ma'am, we have to carry on our investigation right now," Tara said. She glanced up at the sidewalk, here on the main road through town, and her heart faltered in her chest. There were several other local residents up there, people she recognized. They were all standing in some stance of disbelief or anger, their arms folded over their chests or their hands on their hips. Tara hadn't ever seen any of them look at her like that, not all together.

"But it's not right," Lydia said firmly. "Tara…"

"That's Deputy Sheriff Strong," Tara said, even more firmly, meeting her eyes. "Ma'am, I need you to step back from the car. You're obstructing an investigation right now."

The shock of it seemed to get through to Lydia. Tara felt a moment of regret at the look of betrayal on the woman's face. It was something she was probably going to have to fix later. But for now, there was nothing she could do. They were trying to solve a murder. Delicate hurt feelings didn't come into it.

Glenn sped away as Lydia stepped back, and Tara felt relief that they were on the road again. Clearly, the word was out. They needed to get to Tim Weston before the word reached him.

"How did she know?" Glenn asked, his voice tense.

Tara glanced at him. He really didn't realize? "You said his name on the radio," she told him.

Glenn's face flickered through a number of emotions, most of them negative. Guilt seemed to win out. "I was just talking to the Sheriff," he said.

"Yes," Tara replied. "But you never know who else might be listening."

"Lesson learned," Glenn muttered,

They took the road that led out of town and up towards the lake. The scenery flashed by as Glenn gunned it, switching on the siren whenever they came up behind slow-moving traffic so they could blitz past. The miles disappeared quickly under the wheels of the car, until they were entering the shadowed lane that led along the side of the lake with trees lining the other side. Tara felt the tension growing, shifting uncomfortably in her seat.

They were about to confront a man who she thought could be a killer. That was serious. This was probably the most dangerous thing she had ever been called on to do, and they couldn't even spare anyone to provide backup.

It was also the most thrilling thing she had ever done.

"Here it is," Glenn said, starting to slow the car as a cabin appeared in the near distance, and Tara found herself reaching for the gun at her hip.

CHAPTER FIFTEEN

"There's nothing," Tara said, calling over to Glenn. She wiped the back of a hand across her forehead. She was getting more and more uncomfortable by the minute.

Glenn emerged from behind the cabin, walking back around toward her. He shook his head. "No one's home. He's not just hiding in there. I looked through all the windows."

"He could have locked himself in the bathroom," Tara suggested.

"No, the door's open," Glenn replied. "And there's more. I could see a couple of guns up on the wall. Three mounts, two guns."

"He's got one with him," Tara translated.

"He's probably out there hunting," Glenn said. "From what I know, he covers the area pretty nearby. Far enough from the cabin that the wildlife isn't afraid to walk, and not much further."

Tara nodded, thinking carefully. They couldn't just go and come back. If they did, Weston would have time to hear about the fact they were after him and get out of Dodge. Not to mention that he could destroy any evidence that might be in the small three-room cabin.

It was a small cabin, now that Tara thought of that. A bedroom, open-plan living space, and a bathroom. Was there space in there for what Miley Piper had described? Was it clean enough, tidy enough, to represent that empty bedroom she had talked about?

There was no point in debating that with herself now. She had to make a decision. Bring Tim Weston in one way or another and see what he had to say, protect the evidence, and then figure it out from there.

"We have to find him," she said. Part of her was reluctant to suggest it, but what choice did they have? "We'll head into the woods and split up."

"Split up?" Glenn started. His brown eyes opened wide. "Tara, do you think that's wise?"

"What would be unwise would be going through the woods together and letting him easily slip past us back to the cabin," Tara countered. "We've got to bring him in, Glenn. That's what matters right now. If we can't find him, we'll go from there."

Glenn once again looked like he was swallowing back an objection, trying to respect her decision. He nodded curtly. "Guns out though, right?"

"Keep it pointed low," Tara advised. "We don't want any accidents. And if you see a particular shade of olive green, for God's sake, don't shoot."

Glenn smirked at her last warning, a reference to the color of their uniforms. "I won't shoot you."

"Good," Tara said, then pointed in the direction of the trees. "You go that way; I'll go this way. Once you find him, if you do, holler. I'll do the same."

Glenn nodded again, clenched his jaw, and then turned to walk in the direction she had indicated. In a funny kind of way, seeing him ignore his nerves to get the job done enabled Tara to do the same. After sending him off into the woods, she couldn't exactly refuse to go herself. She squared her shoulders and walked forward, heading right between the trees.

Once she was a few feet away from the cabin, everything changed. It was always that way when walking into the trees. The open, loud, and manmade world they had been inhabiting disappeared. They were far enough away from the rest of the habitation around the lake to avoid even the sound of vehicles, and instead Tara plunged into a world of birds and small animals. All she could hear around her was birdsong and rustling, creatures or else the breeze moving the leaves to rub together in the air.

She looked to the side and saw Glenn moving quietly through the trees, his gaze focused ahead. He had his gun drawn and pointed low at the ground. He looked back and saw her and nodded once before moving on. Before long, if she carried on moving at the angle she had chosen, they would lose sight of one another.

Tara swallowed and drew her own gun.

She took more careful steps through the trees, straining all of her senses. She heard a distant crunch as Glenn stepped on a twig and broke it. Her eyes flicked back and forth constantly, straining for a flash of color.

She was walking through hunting grounds. It occurred to her, far too late, that you were supposed to wear bright orange if you were walking through hunting grounds, to avoid becoming game yourself. But if she wore orange now, Tim Weston would see her coming easily. He would know where she was before she even saw him, most likely, given his experience as a hunter compared to her own. It was a lose-lose situation.

If he was the killer, she wanted to make sure he didn't see her until she was right on him. That was the only way she was going to manage to bring him in single-handedly, with Glenn probably too far away to make a difference if Weston decided to run or fight her.

Was this a mistake?

If it was, it would be too late to correct it. Tara kept on walking, trying to ignore the gnawing feeling in her gut that was growing stronger with every second. She couldn't go back now. If she did, she would leave Glenn on his own out here, with no way to call him back that wouldn't involve loudly announcing his whereabouts to anyone nearby – probably leaving him in even more danger.

She couldn't turn back.

She –

Tara reacted bodily to the sound of a shot ringing out, a millisecond later impacting a tree close to her left. She didn't turn around to see the bullet hole. She had heard the bark fly up, and that was enough. Someone was firing at her. She couldn't waste a moment. She turned and fired back in the direction the shot had come from and heard a male voice cry out in response, only just audible in the ringing that filled her ears post-shot.

She dodged to the side now the shot was done, trying to get a vantage point through the trees. She heard someone moving off further to the left – Glenn, she thought, rushing through the woods towards them. He was basically announcing his presence, running so loudly that there wasn't a person or beast in the woods who would have mistaken him. There was no use in staying stealthy if her partner ended up getting shot next. Tara gritted her teeth and rushed forward, too, keeping her gun in her hand in case she needed to use it again.

She saw glimpses through the trees and recognized Tim Weston, his face gritted in pain as she got close enough to spot him on the ground. Glenn was converging on the same spot, and when she saw Weston lift his gun and point it in Glenn's direction, Tara felt her heart actually stop. She gasped in relief when Weston relaxed and dropped the gun as Glenn emerged into sight, Weston no doubt recognizing his Sheriff's uniform.

Tara was there only a second later, reaching them in time to see Weston push the gun in Glenn's direction, allowing him to pick it up to be sure the man was completely disarmed.

"Hands in the air, Weston," Tara said, between pants for breath.

Weston just looked at her for a long moment. He raised his hands with a sharp intake of breath, and Tara saw why he seemed to have such anger in his gaze. One of them was heavily stained with red blood.

"This is Deputy Grayson calling in a ten-seventy-one," he said. *Send an ambulance.* "We have a suspect with a gunshot wound in his lower leg."

"Tim Weston," Tara said, her heart pounding, knowing she needed to caution him now so that anything he might say in the ambulance or the hospital would count as part of his interview. "You're under arrest on suspicion of attempted murder."

***

"Alright," Tara said, settling into the chair beside Tim Weston's county hospital bed. He glared at her from his seated position, his newly-wrapped leg propped up in front of him. Glenn stood behind her, like a bodyguard waiting to be called into action. "Let's start with what you were doing in the woods."

"I was hunting," Weston snapped. "I have a permit. I'm allowed to do that."

"And do you mind explaining why you shot at someone wearing a Sheriff's department uniform?" Tara asked icily, matching his tone. She didn't mention the fact that *she* was the one wearing the uniform. She didn't want to make it sound like this was personal.

"I saw a deer," Weston said. "Or at least, I thought I saw a deer. I saw movement and something a kind of brown color. That's what I was there to hunt, so I fired."

"You fired without confirming what it was you were looking at?" Tara challenged.

"You ever been hunting, girl?" Weston asked, looking her up and down distastefully.

"Funnily enough, I have more important things to do with my time," Tara said. "Like hunting killers."

Tim Weston barked a laugh. "Killers? Ain't been anything more than a spot of poaching going on in this county since before you were born. Don't make yourself out to be something special, 'cause you're not."

"We've had more than a few disappearances," Tara pointed out, gritting her teeth to ignore the personal barb. He was trying to get a rise out of her, throwing his weight around to show how superior he was. "What do you have to say about those?"

He snorted. "You think I had something to do with that sweet sister of yours?" He grinned wide, showing a few brown teeth. "Believe me, if she was my girl, she wouldn't be in hiding. She'd be out lording it around in town bragging about how she caught the biggest and best man in Edgar County." He made a crude thrust with his hips, and the fact that he winced right afterwards in pain was only partial compensation. Tara clenched her fists, trying to will herself not to attack him right there in the bed.

"Let's get back to the matter at hand, shall we?" Glenn asked, with a calm that Tara couldn't understand he was capable of at that moment. "You say you thought you saw a deer."

"Yeah, and then you shot me!" Weston exclaimed, gesturing angrily at Tara. "You crazy bitch! I was just hunting, and you shot me in the damn leg!"

"It's our policy to return fire," Tara explained as calmly as she could. "You shouldn't have shot towards a member of the Sheriff's department. Given we were there to actively bring you in on suspicion of attempted murder and abduction, we had to assume you were hostile." She was starting to get the feeling that she was overexplaining – that he didn't need this level of detail – but the urge to defend herself was high.

"I'm going to sue you for this," he snapped. "Loss of earnings, emotional trauma, and the hospital bills – plus gross negligence or whatever they might call it. You better hope they give you a good lawyer, not just one of the briefs the county keeps around for defendants. I'm going to come after your job, your pension, and the whole department."

Tara ignored that, too, just like she ignored everything he tried to goad or threaten her with. Dealing with people like Tim Weston required an awful lot of turning the other cheek, which she was not traditionally good at. But with a case like this, it mattered too much for her to let him get to her. They needed answers. They needed to find out who had killed those girls, and if it was Tim Weston, then she wasn't going to let him distract her with nonsense about litigation.

She was pretty sure he wouldn't win if he brought a case against her, anyway.

"Where were you on Sunday evening?" Tara asked. They needed to cut through to the meat of this. There was no point trying to reason with a man who had no logic or reasoning.

"What?" Tim Weston looked between Glenn and Tara, as if the man in the room was going to give him more answers. "Wait, you were going to arrest me for murder before I shot at you?"

It was becoming very clear that Tim Weston was more than a little slow on the uptake. "Yes," Tara said. "Now, answer the question."

"I was with my brother, Donny," he said.

"Where?" Tara asked. Getting information from him was like pulling teeth. Not only was it painful, but it apparently had to be done one piece at a time.

"At the cabin," Tim said. "It's Donny's cabin. I'm just living there."

"Doing what?" Tara asked through clenched teeth, wishing he would actually give her the answers she obviously needed. Unless he was deliberately trying to obfuscate so they wouldn't look too hard into the alibi, he was doing a terrible job of clearing his name.

"We were drinking," Weston shrugged. "Shooting our mouths off. Donny's fighting with his old lady, so he came over to bitch to me about it."

Tara just held off rolling her eyes at the colorful language. "Anyone else who can uphold this alibi, other than your own brother?" she asked, trying to state the obvious with her tone. Donny would lie for Tim, no questions asked. The Westons had each other's backs. They had to, for the amount of times one or the other of them had been in trouble with the law.

"No," Weston shrugged. "You saw it right before you barged into my woods with your police brutality and shot me. We're isolated. No one can see us up there."

Tara noted that down in the *no proof* column. On the other hand, she was starting to have a bad feeling about Tim Weston's status as a suspect. For one thing, her interactions with him and his brothers over the years had left her with the impression that he didn't have the intelligence to pull off a good lie. For another, the size of that cabin was a worry. It didn't fit with what she had imagined from Miley Piper's description. And given that she said she'd smashed a window, he would have needed to repair it pretty quickly – Tara didn't recall seeing as much of a twinkle of broken glass catching the light on the ground. Given he wasn't the most houseproud of cabin owners, she doubted he would have done more than put a piece of cardboard over the hole and duct-taped it in place.

They needed more, though. All she had was an unproven alibi and an unproven suspicion.

"What can you tell me about your movements for the last seven years?" she asked, going a year back beyond their oldest-dated victim to see if she could throw him off. "Have you had access to the cabin for all of that time?"

Tim shook his head. "Donny bought it five years back," he said. "When Gramps died and left us some cash. Anyway, I wasn't around here back then."

"No?" Tara asked, her eyes narrowing. Was that true? She tried to think back. "Where were you?"

"I was with Gramps," Tim said. "I stayed with him until he died. I was with him for a couple of years."

Five years ago, plus two – that implied that Tim hadn't been around when Ness Griffin was killed. "But you came back to town occasionally," Tara said, trying to catch him out.

"Nope," Tim said, folding his arms over his chest. "Me and Donny was fighting back then because he wanted to look after Gramps. He thought I was going to get all the money. When Gramps died and we both got some, we started talking again, and that's when I came back to town."

It was a kind of vague alibi. How could they check every night of his whereabouts over a two-year period?

"I kind of remember that," Glenn said slowly. "About five years ago, when he first came back into town."

"Oh, yeah?" Tim asked, wiggling his eyebrows up and down. "You had some kind of candle for me, darlin'?"

That word again.

"No, we just make sure we're all aware of anyone who has a criminal record who lives in the county," Tara said flatly, making sure to drive her point home as carefully as possible. She didn't want him getting any other ideas and trying to add some kind of sexual harassment claim to his suit. "Are you sure?" This last part was angled up over her shoulder, aimed at Glenn.

"Yeah," he nodded. He looked apologetic. "I remember. It was the first time he'd been seen in town. Maybe that doesn't say anything about the cabin, though."

"We didn't have the cabin," Tim said, rolling his eyes. "Do I have to spell it out for you?"

He was rich, trying to talk as though they were the ones who were slow to get the message. But it was a strong point. If he didn't even have the cabin back then, and he didn't have a home in town, how could he have found somewhere to keep the girls? It was becoming more and more likely that they were simply wrong about Tim Weston.

He was an asshole, but he wasn't a killer.

Just like everyone else had said. Tara tried not to let that get to her.

"Alright," she said, standing up. "You're still under arrest. Until we've thoroughly investigated your alibi, you have to stay here."

"It's not like I'm going anywhere," he scoffed, gesturing to his leg. "Anyway, *you* better not go anywhere. Because I'm suing you."

"I'll tell you what, Mr. Weston," Tara said, faux-breezily, turning to go but addressing him over her shoulder. "You don't sue me, and I won't charge you for attempting to murder a Deputy Sheriff. Deal?"

Weston had the good sense to clear his throat and look sheepish. "Deal."

"Let's get out of here," Tara said to Glenn, taking him with her as she walked out of the ward. In the main hallway of the hospital, the windows showed the early evening, the sun dipping down toward twilight. "We've got to start again from scratch – before the real killer, whoever he is, decides he wants a new girl to replace the one he lost."

"From scratch?" Glenn groaned. "We need some kind of lead to narrow things down, or we're never going to get there."

"We have one," Tara said, remembering the thought she'd had about the cabin. "Windows. We need to look for broken windows – and whether anyone has bought the materials in town to repair one."

CHAPTER SIXTEEN

Rosalyn examined herself in the mirror, running her fingers over the delicate skin under her eyes and turning her head this way and that, trying to figure out whether she was showing any signs of aging. She'd heard that using moisturizer on your face from an early age could really help, and she'd been a religious daily user since she was sixteen. It was paying off, she thought.

Okay, maybe she was only twenty-one and there weren't likely to be many signs of aging yet, but she had friends who were starting to look worse for wear. Tiny crow's feet and black bags, even patches of unevenly colored skin near their eyes from being out in the sun all summer long. Rosalyn, however, was pleased to see she didn't have any of those signs at all. She blinked her large green eyes at herself in the mirror, fanning her lash extensions, and grinned.

She looked great for her date tonight.

As a last touch, she reached for a small pot of lip gloss under the mirror and dabbed it onto her lips, smacking them together to make sure it was evenly spread. She grinned again and then turned, glancing around the house for whatever else needed to be done before Todd got home from work.

There was trash by the back door waiting to be taken out. That would be a good start. There had been too much taking out the trash, cleaning the floors, and making the bed since she and Todd had moved in together and not enough dates. Hopefully, tonight would be the start of fixing that.

"You don't know what you're missing, Todd Tatton," Rosalyn muttered out loud to herself, just for her own amusement. That had been what she'd said to him the day she had asked him why on earth he had never bothered to ask her out, and he'd said he thought they were just friends. That had done the trick. Kind of. It had taken a while to filter through his head, but finally a week later he had asked her out after all, and then everything had gone kind of fast.

A message alert interrupted her on her way to the back door, and Rosalyn paused to read a message from her best friend.

Can't believe about this crazy guy going around snatching girls off the street. Watch out sis!! x

Rosalyn shook her head, thinking about how awful it was that someone had been abducted recently. You didn't hear about that kind of thing out here in Edgar County. You just didn't. And the fact that it had happened so close by, too – it was just awful.

Don't worry. I'm out w Todd tonight! Not going anywhere on my own. U shouldn't either x

She slipped the cell phone back into her back pocket and hefted the trash bag, grimacing as the weight shifted and something clinked. She didn't want anything nasty to spill out onto the floor before she could get it out to the trash cans outside of the little house they rented. That would mean cleaning, and she sure as hell wasn't getting down on her hands and knees to scrub the floor in her new red date night dress. Not before Todd had seen it in all its glory, anyway.

She opened the door and headed out to the backyard, taking the hard left along the side of the house. She left the back door open – she was only going to be gone a minute, and this was a safe neighborhood, so it wasn't even a thought.

She threw the bag into the trash can with a clunk, hearing the rustle of the plastic settling into place. She dusted off her hands and then gasped – was that a chip on one of her nails? She rushed back around the corner and into the house, wanting to check it in the light.

She breathed out. It was fine. She'd only just had them done that morning ready for date night – it would have been awful if they'd been chipped already. She turned and closed the back door, taking a breath. Nearly perfect. Everything was nearly perfect. Now Todd just had to get home from work, and they could begin.

She sighed happily, walking over to the other side of the room, and passing by the darkness of the open bedroom door.

Something grabbed her by the waist, and she found herself screaming – a sound that was cut off as whoever it was yanked her head back. Rosalyn knew instinctively that it wasn't just Todd playing a joke on her. There was no way he would ever be this rough – ever hurt her intentionally.

And if it wasn't Todd, then she had to get away from whoever it was.

She threw her elbow back, fighting to free herself from his arms. She felt rather than knew it was a he – the strength, then height – and when the elbow didn't work, she aimed a kick behind herself and up, trying to catch something that would make him stop. She felt her foot collide with something – maybe a thigh – but not nearly hard enough. Her elbow sawed through the air, hitting him in the chest and stomach over and over again until finally –

He let go. For a second, she felt it. He was no longer holding her in place. She hit the ground and pushed herself forward, stretching towards the front door, thinking that she could run –

And something hit her, hard, over the head, and she fell to the floor.

She rolled over and looked up at him, trying to see who he was at least – but before she could react, he hit her again, and she felt her world going black.

CHAPTER SEVENTEEN

Tara eyed the other car in the Sheriff's parking lot warily as they pulled in. "Why are they here?" she asked.

Glenn glanced over, cutting off the engine. "State police," he said. "Huh. Don't suppose you think there's any chance they're here about another case?"

"It would have to be one hell of a coincidence," Tara said. She took off her seatbelt and got out of the car, looking around the lot as if she was expecting another armed suspect to pop up at any moment. Having the state police show up wasn't exactly the same kind of threat – but it was still a threat, all the same.

"Whose car is that?" Glenn asked, nodding towards the far side of the parking lot at a civilian vehicle.

Tara looked at it, squinting, trying to pull through her memory and see if she recognized it.

"I don't know," she said, but she had a sinking feeling, as if this was a car she already knew was related to something that wasn't good at all.

Then she placed it.

"Oh, God," she muttered.

"It's not, is it?" Glenn asked. She looked at him. His brown eyes were wide under his curly brown hair, and his jaw had dropped. He must have realized just at the same moment she had.

"But I really must insist!" Lydia Peablossom's voice rang out, and they both turned to see her being ushered out of the Sheriff's station by a determined-looking Deputy Bryant. He'd been left on his own since they weren't there, and he was still manning the phones – he must have had to come out to help the receptionist get rid of Lydia.

"Even if you insist," Bryant said flatly. "I'm sorry, ma'am. We have an active investigation right now. Unless you have a witness statement to provide or you need to report a different crime, please stay clear of the Sheriff's station."

“Do you need a hand, Deputy?” Glenn asked, speaking up deliberately as they approached.

Lydia Peablossom looked around, realizing that she was about to be much more outnumbered. Her mouth flattened into a line of frustration and then she seemingly gave up, flapping her hands toward Bryant as if to tell him he didn’t need to shoo her.

“Fine, fine,” she muttered, walking away. “But I told them not to arrest one of us.”

Tara and Glenn exchanged a glance, and the two of them followed Bryant quickly into the station before they could get caught up in another discussion with the ever-persistent Lydia.

The relief when the door closed safely behind them was incredibly short-lived.

“Tara!” Braddock barked. “Get over here right now!”

Tara took a deep breath and met Glenn’s eyes again. When he raised an eyebrow, she shook her head. She would face Braddock alone.

The downside to being the Sheriff's favored deputy was the fact that she was not only singled out for rewards and opportunities, but also for punishments.

Tara walked across the near-empty office towards Braddock’s private office at the far end, going in without a word and closing the door behind her. She thought about sitting down and then decided not to. She felt she would be in a stronger position if she stayed this way.

“I’ve just been out at the lake overseeing the digging efforts,” Braddock half-shouted, his hands on his hips as he stood behind his desk looking down at her. “Can you tell me why in the hell I’ve been called back here to deal with the paperwork over one of my officers shooting a civilian?”

“He shot at us first,” Tara said immediately. She felt it was important to get the mitigating circumstances out of the way first. “He pointed a loaded weapon at me and fired. We can retrieve the spent casing and the bullet from the tree it went into.”

“And I’m supposed to spare someone to go and collect that now, am I?” Sheriff Braddock demanded. “In the middle of what looks to be shaping into a serial murder case?”

“I’m sorry,” Tara said. “But that’s just the thing. This is a serious case, and we knew that. If he was the killer, and he was firing at us – I had to take him down and stop him from killing anyone else. And I only shot him in the leg."

"By luck, from what I hear." Braddock said, blowing air heavily out of his nose. He paced a step or two behind his desk in the small amount of space available, looking like he wanted to charge toward a red cloak.

There was a light knock at the window, almost as if someone didn't want to interrupt their conversation, and both Tara and the Sheriff looked around to see Glenn standing there on the other side of the glass. He wasn't far from his desk, and Tara figured he'd either heard Braddock shouting or was reading lips through the clear window. Once he saw he had their attention, he raised up two plastic evidence bags in front of the glass. One of them held a bullet, and the other held a shell casing.

He must have dug them out while Tara was preoccupied with flagging down the ambulance, hearing the ringing in her ears from the gunshot.

"Once again, Deputy Grayson saves your hide," Sheriff Braddock muttered, shaking his head. He made a dismissive gesture toward Glenn and snapped the blinds shut, leaving Tara alone with him in their conversation. "You can't keep going off half-cocked, Tara. If you can only function properly with Grayson at your side, then maybe he should be the one training for my job."

Tara felt her face blanch in spite of her best efforts. He wouldn't take her job away, would he? The thought of Jessy's face flashed through her mind and she clenched her fists at her side. She couldn't let that happen.

"I won't let you down again," she said, her voice tightly controlled, every word enunciated carefully.

"You better not," Braddock said wearily. He was looking at her with that look he often had. The one that her father also wore when she did something bad. It said he cared for and believed in her, but she had disappointed him again. "I've got the state police here trying to take over the case, telling me they don't think our department is capable of handling something on this scale."

Now her heart dropped like a stone into her stomach, leaving Tara feeling cold. If they lost the investigation because of her, it wasn't just her own career that would be affected. And she wouldn't have the opportunity to keep on with the case, seeing it through to the end – something she desperately wanted. Not only that, but she'd begun to build a rapport with Miley Piper – and if someone else took over the investigation, they might have to destroy her fragile trust by switching to someone new.

When she was there with her, Tara had to imagine herself interviewing her own sister. Interviewing Cassie, as if she was the one who had run screaming out of the woods. She couldn't bear it now if someone else took over, someone else who might not realize the gentler touch that Miley Piper needed.

"I'm sorry," she said to the floor. "I'm really sorry. I didn't want to fire at him. It was a defensive maneuver. But next time I'll get backup and find a better way of tracking a suspect down than going into a hunting zone."

"Right," Sheriff Braddock sighed. "You've got another lead to try and follow?"

"Yes," Tara said smartly, lifting her head. At least here, she could show him that she wasn't a total disappointment. "Broken windows. The owner of the cabin either still has a broken window or they've had to repair it – in which case we should be able to follow the trail of the building materials or labor."

"Get back to it," Sherriff Braddock said, dismissing her with another wave of his hand. It wasn't quite an acknowledgement that she'd done a good job by thinking up another angle of attack, but at least he wasn't yelling at her anymore.

Tara quickly exited his office and headed to sit down at her desk with Glenn, who was on the phone. He glanced at her and she pulled a face, then smiled. He nodded, understanding what she was trying to say: she was in trouble, but she'd gotten away with it for now.

"Alright, thanks so much," Glenn said into the phone, catching Tara's attention. At the other end of the room, Deputy Bryant was also on the phone, and she tried to tune him out. He was probably taking another tip from the rumor mill of Wyatt's residents. "And do get in touch with us if anyone comes in. Thanks."

He put the phone down and sighed, which was never a good sign.

"Who was that?" Tara asked.

"The last of the DIY stores in town," he said. "While you were in there, I called both of them and also Hank Mayfield. He said no one's hired him or even asked about repairing windows, and they haven't sold any supplies that would make sense either. And Hank asked me if he should be telling me about any out-of-towners that come through –

sounds like the whole town is starting to grow suspicious of outsiders, not believing it could be one of us."

"Great." It was Tara's turn to sigh. "Another dead end."

"We can still use it to narrow down cabins," Glenn suggested brightly. "Maybe we can drive around and look at properties, you know. Spot the one with the broken window."

"That could take hours," Tara said, then corrected herself. "No – if we go around the more remote ones, days."

"Whatever it takes," Glenn shrugged, half-hopefully, like he really wanted her to think his suggestion was a good one.

"We should try to -" Tara stopped, cut off by Bryant's voice from the other side of the room.

"Sheriff!" he yelled, and Tara and Glenn gave him her full attention even as Sheriff Braddock burst out of his office.

"What is it?" Braddock demanded, seeing how wild Bryant's face looked.

"There's a missing woman," Bryant said, words that sent tongues of icy-cold fire down Tara's spine. "Her boyfriend just called us – she's supposed to meet him after work to go on a date, but the place is a mess, things knocked over, the door left open. He said it looks like she's been taken."

"Let's go," Sheriff Braddock said, storming toward the door and beckoning curtly for Tara and Glenn to go with him.

CHAPTER EIGHTEEN

Tara stood in the wreckage of the home Rosalyn Clement shared with her boyfriend, Todd Tatton, wondering if this was the kind of mess that you made when you killed someone in their own home.

A vase of flowers had been knocked to the ground and smashed. The flowers themselves had been trampled into the carpet, though only in patches – not enough, sadly, to provide a footprint. The harsh lights of the home's interior, holding at bay the darkness of the evening that had drawn down on them rapidly, showed splashes of water across the carpet. A table had been knocked askew with the chairs tipped over beside it, as if someone had knocked into it hard. A shoe, red and strappy with a tall heel, lay on the carpet, discarded, one of the straps broken.

"She would never have left her cell phone behind," Todd said despondently, practically wringing his hands as he held the item up. "She would never go anywhere without it."

Tara wished he hadn't picked it up, given that he had most probably obscured any existing fingerprints by doing so, but he was clearly distraught. His eyes were wide and searching around in all directions under unruly blonde hair that stuck up at weird angles, as though he had grabbed it with his fingers and pulled.

"Alright, Mr. Tatton," Sheriff Braddock said. "Just tell us step by step what happened when you came home from your late shift."

"I was running late," he said, robotically, as if a memory had been triggered by the keyword of late. "I was supposed to be here for our date night and I thought she might be mad at me. I came rushing in. I unlocked the door and I called out 'Sorry, babe' as I came in. But I looked down and it was… like this."

"Did you touch anything else?" Tara asked. "It's very important for us to know."

"No, I just – I picked up her phone," he said. "I thought I might… I don't know. See something. Like a clue. But there's nothing. And then

I realized I can't call her to find out where she is, because I have her phone right here."

"We'll find her, Mr. Tatton," Glenn reassured him, and Tara turned to give him a glare behind Todd's back. That wasn't something you should ever say to the relatives of people who were missing. She knew firsthand that such a thing simply wasn't possible to guarantee.

"Do you know of anyone who had been hanging around lately?" Sheriff Braddock asked. "Did she talk about anyone watching her, or showing up at work? Anyone new, or even someone who's been around for a while?"

Todd shook his head slowly. "No, man. Are you trying to say you think…?"

"We've got to assume she's been taken by a third party at this point," Sheriff Braddock said. "I'm sorry, son, but it doesn't look like she left here willingly."

"But is it…" Todd lowered his voice, whispered, glancing around. "Him?"

"Him?" Glenn repeated, but Tara had a very strong idea that she knew who he was talking about already.

"The man who took that other girl," Todd said. He looked at all three of them for answers, his eyes wide and his jaw slack as he contemplated the possibility. He was, quite clearly, terrified at the idea of losing someone that he cared for a great deal.

"We can't speculate just yet," Sheriff Braddock said. He lowered his voice. "But it's a very real possibility. Just help us do our jobs, son. That's the best thing you can do now."

"Is he going to kill her?" Todd asked, his bottom lip quivering.

"Not tonight," Tara said, her mouth dry.

There was only one witness statement they had to rely on. That was Miley Piper's statement. She'd said she had been held overnight and told the next evening that she was set to die. There was no way of knowing whether he had intended to kill her right away or kill her a little while later after that – no evidence that the graves could give them, given how old they were. There was nothing to say that one day or two days was the norm. Maybe he kept some for weeks and others for just a day.

But Tara believed what Miley had told her. Everything else Miley had said rang true – the dog tag, the connection to the lake. They knew for a fact that the cabin was somewhere through the trees because that was where she had run from, and the twigs and leaves stuck to her clothing bore it out. So, it stood to reason that she was also right about the passage of time while she was in the cabin.

Overnight, Tara felt she could say with some confidence that Rosalyn Clement was still alive. In the morning, that certainty dropped. And in the evening, she felt sure that if Rosalyn wasn't dead already, her minutes would be numbered.

There was a ticking clock hanging over their heads now – and if they didn't manage to put everything together to catch this killer within the next twenty-four hours, Tara felt sure that there would be one more body to add to the list.

"I'm going back to talk to our witness," Tara said, announcing it as a statement but also partially hoping that Sheriff Braddock would nod his approval and give her permission.

"Someone saw her get taken?" Todd asked, with hope that made Tara feel awful.

"No," she said, watching him revert back into his former crushed self. "A witness to the man who abducted someone a couple of days ago. I'm going back to the hospital."

She had to talk to Miley Piper again – and see if there was anything the young woman could tell them which would put them on the track of this killer.

***

Tara set a cup of lukewarm decaf coffee down on the table by the bed, smiling warmly at Miley as she did. Their escaped victim had improved a little since their last talk, it seemed – a little more color in her cheeks had appeared over the last day, and she was sitting up. She had looked directly at Tara when she entered the room and hadn't cringed away.

"How are you feeling?" Tara asked. It would have been quicker to get to the point, to ask what she needed to know. But there was no rushing this, Tara had learned. She needed to play the long game. Be kind, warm, ask after her health. If she seemed more mentally up to it, the harder questions could come later.

"I'm much better, thank you," Miley said. Even her speech seemed clearer. Tara thought she had washed and brushed her hair, too, taking advantage of the private bathroom attached to the room. "I just had dinner. And it's not like what they say. The food's not bad here at all."

Tara grinned. "That's good news," she said, sitting down on the chair next to the bed. It was cold, still, but she thought she felt a ghost of heat from maybe a short while before. "I heard your family have been here to see you, too."

Miley nodded confirmation, ducking her head to look down at her hands. "They don't quite understand, but… it's nice that they're here." She looked up again at Tara. "Visiting hours finished, so they went home. The nurses wouldn't let them stay. I guess you're the exception."

Tara chuckled, tapping the badge on her uniform. "This thing gets us a few perks," she said. "Being able to visit outside of hours is just one of them."

"You must be here to ask me more questions," Miley said. She had a perceptive, sharp look to her now. "That's why you're here, isn't it?"

Tara nodded with a light smile. "Sorry," she said. "I didn't have time for a social visit today. We've been busy investigating. But I would like to chat some more if you're up for it."

Miley nodded, tucking her long red hair behind her ears. Her green eyes peeked at Tara, who couldn't help thinking of the other girls. Those green eyes had got her into a lot of trouble, through no actual fault of their own. Those green eyes were why she had been kidnapped.

"Great," Tara smiled. "We need to go over a few details of your statement. I want you to think hard about the man's voice, first of all."

"Okay," Miley nodded thoughtfully. Her eyes turned up to the ceiling, as if she was bringing it back to her mind.

"Can you be precise about how he sounded?" Tara asked. "His accent – you said it sounded local."

"Yes, he was definitely Coloradan," she replied.

Tara's heart sank a little. Coloradan – not specifically from Wyatt. But it was still something they could work with. She kept thinking about the plate on that truck before she remembered that it didn't actually help at all.

"Is there anything specifically he said that was a little funny, something that you wouldn't expect to hear?" Tara pressed, thinking of the strange ways people here had of saying things sometimes. Things born of the mountain and the lake.

"Not really," Miley said. Then she narrowed her eyes, like she was thinking. "But he did seem a bit strange. Like he didn't talk to other people much."

That was interesting. "Was he very formal?"

"Yes, kind of stiff," Miley said. "I felt like he was unsure of what he said – unsure of whether it was the right way to say things. At first I thought he was apologetic because of what he was going to – to do, but now I think also he was waiting for approval on his words."

"Can you think of anything else that will help us with the location?" Tara asked.

"Oh," Miley said, and then her eyes brightened. "Yes. The cabin – I don't know if it was lived in."

"What do you mean?"

"Well, the covers on the bed – they were very fresh and new. And the pattern was… I don't know how to describe it, really. But it felt like something you would buy for a guest room. And when he was around, there was a smell. Like the woods. I don't think it was aftershave."

"That's interesting," Tara said thoughtfully. Something had triggered in her memory – something that she hadn't thought of at all for a while. Last summer, there was a complaint. A couple of hikers had said they'd seen someone in the woods – someone half-mad, like a wilderness man. After a bit of investigation, Tara and Glenn had dismissed it as a prank. They'd assumed some kids had probably dressed up and had fun scaring tourists. But hadn't they said they saw him up near the northern shore of one of the smaller lakes, about a half-day's hike from where Miley had been found…?

"I think maybe he lived outdoors a lot," Miley said. "You know, from the smell and the awkwardness and the room. Like maybe a lumberjack or something. Do you get lumberjacks up here? Anyway, I thought of something like that. Only living alone, not working with others."

Tara nodded, meeting Miley's eyes with a warm smile. "That's really great," she said. "Well done, Miley. And if you do think of any other details, no matter how small they might be, you can ask the nurses to call me any time."

Miley smiled just slightly, ducking her head as if she was pleased to receive the praise. "Okay," she said. "I'll tell them if I do. I can't wait to get home, though. To have my own phone."

"As soon as you do, let's make sure my number gets programmed in it," Tara said, trying to keep that same air like she was talking to a new friend, making plans for the future.

"Okay," Miley said, nodding.

Tara stood calmly and walked toward the door, nodding and smiling just one last time in farewell at the threshold and waiting for Miley to return the same look before she left.

And then she found Glenn a few steps away in the corridor, and dropped the calm and warm demeanor she had adopted. "Get back to the car," she hissed at him, already moving as fast as she could to lead by example. Short of outright running through the hospital corridors, which could be dangerous, she made an effort to walk as fast as she could.

"What's going on?" Glenn asked, rushing after her to keep up with her sudden appearance.

"You remember our mysterious mountain man from last year?" she asked. "It wasn't a prank. Come on. We've got to go and search that area – and find out where our killer has been hiding. I don't think he's in the cabin at all. I think he lives in the woods and breaks into cabins when he needs them."

Glenn swore under his breath and put on a surge of speed, and by the time they hit the parking lot they were neck and neck, speed-walking toward the car like their lives depended on it.

Because Rosalyn Clement's did.

CHAPTER NINETEEN

The moon was bright overhead as they got out of the car, a fact that Tara was grateful for. It would make things easier to see.

Until they were among the thickest of the trees, where the light from the sun barely penetrated at midday, and the sun had no chance – or until the moon went behind one of the clouds that was waiting to take over.

"Which direction from here?" Glenn asked, his voice hushed. There was almost silence around them, the silence of nature, which was actually made up of a lot of small noises. The whisper of breezes through the leaves of the trees, the murmur as the trees swayed together. The scurry of small creatures through the undergrowth and over the branches, the flapping of wings, the calling of birds already warning friends on the other side of the clearing to watch out for approaching humans. Give it a moment for the sound of the engine to die away and there would be more calls – including those of larger animals, the ones who knew to stay away from things that roared and smelled of gas.

Tara pointed towards the slope of the mountain. It was hidden from them here by the trees, but Tara was born and raised in the shadow of it and she knew which way it was. There was a joke among the locals that there were only three types of directions: away from the mountain, towards the mountain, and past the mountain. "We go that way. If there's any spot we didn't find before that a man could hide in, it would be along the side of the mountain. There are plenty of caves and overhangs that way. We just don't rush in alone. Or at all. Don't forget, these places are home to other things."

"How could I possibly forget?" Glenn muttered back. "I've seen firsthand what happens when you get too close to a bear up here."

Tara swallowed. She remembered what it looked like herself. There had been a pretty dire case a few years back that both of them had seen the results of. A hiker that got too close to a bear cub and invoked the wrath of the momma bear.

And that was if the serial killer didn't get them first.

Tara took her flashlight from her belt and tightened her grip on it, finding it reassuringly solid. The metal was cold, a match to her gun when she took it from her holster.

"Are we going in armed?" Glenn asked, eyeing her hands as he took out his own flashlight.

"Would you rather have a gun in your hand when a mountain lion leaps for your face, or not?" Tara pointed out.

Glenn swallowed and drew his gun.

Tara led the way forward, motioning for Glenn to keep an eye on their rear as they walked. Once they walked under the cover of the trees, the soft moss and coating of decades of dropped leaves and needles almost bouncy under their feet, everything instantly became much quieter. Their steps were muted, though Tara knew that they would still sound loud as gunshots to many of the animals around them. An owl hooted somewhere overhead – a warning or a hello, Tara couldn't tell.

They kept the base of the mountain to their left, though it wasn't as though there was a firm line between what was and what was not mountain. The ground all around them was rocky, the result of boulders and rocks rolling down from the larger formation over time, and rock still grew from the earth in places here and there. Trees and tree roots overlapped in the space, necessitating a constant watch on their footing.

It was slow going. Tara froze when Glenn stepped on a raised root and snapped it in half with a loud bang, holding up a hand to keep him still as they both examined the trees all around them for signs of movement. When there wasn't any, Tara finally beckoned them forward, though it was strong in her mind that any person who was around them just had a clear warning of their approach.

Then she stopped again, because she had seen something completely incongruous in the context of the thick forest.

Across a half-fallen branch not too far away, there was a forest-green sweater hanging as if drying after being washed.

Tara turned and looked at Glenn, beckoning him forward and pointing. Instead of reacting in surprise as she had expected, he tapped her arm in return and then pointed.

There was a pair of thick woolen socks hanging from a branch on a tree to their right.

Someone was here.

Tara held up a hand with two fingers raised and rocked them forward twice, indicating that they should proceed forward – though silently. Glenn nodded and turned his eyes back toward the mountain. There was thick tree growth here and the rock seemed to rise almost out of the middle of them. They stepped forward, slow and careful, taking the only path that seemed open, edging along the side of the rock.

And then it opened up into a space where a few feet of soil was clear of trees, and in the rock a jagged opening led into a cave.

Tara kept her flashlight pointed at the ground and then, after a moment's thought, switched it off. Glenn did the same. The moonlight shone straight down here and their eyes slowly adjusted to the darkness. The gray rock seemed to almost glow in the pale beams, making the inside of the cave even harder to see.

Tara hesitated. They couldn't discuss it – not this close. They couldn't risk making a sound. She had to make a decision right now, on her own, about what to do.

They had to go in, didn't they?

Tara lifted her gun and pointed it forward, looking at Glenn until she saw he had done the same. She held her flashlight against it as they had been trained but left it turned off, then advanced several slow and painstakingly silent steps to the cave's entrance. Even from here, it was too dark to see more than a handful of inches inside.

Tara looked over and met Glenn's eyes. He nodded, a move she could barely make out. There wasn't an opportunity to count out loud, and her hands were too full to do a visual countdown. There was just what they could communicate with their eyes.

Tara flashed her eyes at him as best she could and then looked forward, turning on her flashlight and charging into the cave.

The first things she saw were other items of clothing and empty packaging from food scattered around the entrance to the cave, a few feet in. It was even more of a clear sign to her that the habitant here was human, not animal. Things weren't scattered randomly, mauled, and chewed. There was order. She took a corner into the larger, more open space of the cave itself and there he was, lying on a camping bed that had been arranged at the back of the space, surrounded by odds and ends of life.

"Freeze!" Tara shouted – a warning that at first seemed unnecessary, since he was not moving at all. But on her shout and with the light, he woke up, staring around at them and beginning to shout what sounded to Tara like gibberish.

All hell broke loose. The circles of light cast by Tara and Glenn's flashlights danced and ricocheted over the walls of the cave as they both angled their guns at him, and the man in the cave leapt out of the bed so fast neither of them managed to react in time. They sought him with their lights, the only way they could see anything at all in the pitch dark and cramped space, sending shadows leaping and jumping over the walls. Something squeaked, and Glenn's light caught a huge rat running for the exit at the same time as Tara's light found their man making a break towards the opposite end of the naturally-formed room.

"Stop!" Tara shouted again. "We're with the Sheriff's department!"

The man yelled something back – again, something she couldn't understand. Tara took a step toward him, her heart racing at the sight of him. He was dirty, his hair matted and unkempt; his clothes were layers on layers of ragged fabric that seemed to be composed largely of holes.

"We're going to take you in to answer some of our questions," Tara said, trying to speak clearly even as she spoke urgently, trying to get him to understand. She took another step forward –

And he launched himself towards her, succeeding in knocking her flat on her back on the floor of the cave. There was no time, no room for her to fire her gun, and the wind was knocked out of her as she landed. It was a miracle she didn't accidentally fire off a shot into the air.

"Hey!" Glenn yelled, rushing forward – but Tara knew that the cave man could do exactly the same thing again in these close quarters, and once he was out in the wilderness he would be gone. This was his forest, his home. He knew well enough that he could disappear from them in the dark and they wouldn't find him again for days – maybe years. Maybe never.

She twisted from her position on the floor, made the split-second decision to risk dropping her gun and her flashlight, and grabbed the man's ankles.

He fell before he could finish lunging for Glenn, making a wheezing grunt as he hit the ground, losing his breath to the hard rock just as she had. Glenn leapt on him immediately, pinning his arms to preclude the idea of any further struggle or the chance for him to run.

"You're under arrest," Tara said, breathing hard.

But what for?

She racked her brain quickly, knowing they didn't have a lot to go on. But it seemed like the man was living out here in the wilderness, in the cave, which would be illegal given that he didn't seem likely to have a permit for anything in particular. There seemed to be a small stove in the cave, and he had to go to the toilet somewhere, and none of this would have been subject to any inspections since nobody knew he was out there. Then there was the matter of who owned the land and whether it had been zoned for habitation or not.

"You're under arrest for illegal use of land and using a cooking stove without a permit," she said, which was a long, wordy charge – but it would work. Hey, they got Al Capone on tax evasion.

And now they'd potentially brought down a serial killer for a stove permit.

"Let's get him to the car," Glenn panted, snapping his handcuffs onto the man's wrists.

And as Glenn tugged him up to his feet, Tara couldn't help but notice one final detail.

The dog tags swinging around their suspect's neck and throwing back the light from her flashlight as they fell from the front of his shirt.

CHAPTER TWENTY

Tara looked through the small square of thick reinforced glass in the window, taking him in, and then stepped away. Their mountain man was sitting in one of the chairs at the interview table, cuffs still on his wrists and a small plastic cup of water in front of him that he hadn't touched.

He looked even worse in the harsh glare of the station lights than he had in front of the flashlights. He looked like he hadn't bathed in months, possibly years, and his clothing could fall apart at any moment. His hair and beard were so thick and matted it was difficult to see his face under and behind them. He was hunched over in the chair, rocking slightly, clearly intensely uncomfortable in his new environment.

"This is going to be difficult," Tara said, overstating the obvious.

"Well, if it gets the results that we need," Sheriff Braddock said. "If this is our man, then we have to nail him. I want you to get a full confession, Tara. I think you can do it, but you'll need to be careful – especially given he's refused his right to an attorney."

Tara nodded. She wasn't sure she felt the full confidence that Braddock was placing in her, but knowing that he had it made her feel better. "I know. No putting words in his mouth."

"Watch your words and don't give him any details that could be used to identify the killer," Braddock said. "Don't mention the dog tags. If he brings that up on his own, we'll know it's him and he won't have a leg to stand on."

"Okay." Tara took a deep breath, trying to psych herself up. "And you'll be watching the video?"

"On the other side of that wall," Braddock said, nodding towards the far end of the interview room. "If he loses it, someone will be with you within seconds."

Tara breathed deeply again. "And you're sure I should do this on my own?" She thought of how he had lunged at her in the cave. She hadn't been able to fight him off, exactly. He was cuffed, but how much damage could he do before someone else rushed in?

"Glenn isn't exactly very threatening, but he's still more threatening than you," Braddock said, which earned him an offended look from Glenn. "I think it's best we continue the successful pattern we've found in dealing with Miley. People trust you, Tara. They can sense you've been through something yourself, and that puts them more at ease. I reckon if you go in there soft, he'll want to talk to you."

Tara took a breath for the third time and nodded. She could do this. She was sure she could. She just needed to fake it until she did.

She opened the door and stepped inside, closing it behind her and moving over to sit in the chair before she could let her nerves betray her. Her hands were shaking, so she folded them onto her lap, sitting back and looking at the mountain man as evenly as she could.

"When can I go back?" he asked, which wasn't the first thing she had expected him to say.

"We need to talk with you first," she said, a cautious answer with no guarantees. "Then we'll look into it."

"I need to go back," he said stubbornly. He refused to look at her. Instead, his eyes roamed across the table, the walls, the floor, anywhere else. It was a kind of creepy mannerism, but the more Tara watched him, the more she thought he was avoiding looking at her out of some kind of fear.

"Why were you up there in the cave?" she asked, thinking she might get somewhere if she took control of the conversation instead of only answering his own questions.

"It's my home," he said. "I have to go back. I have my things."

"I understand that you're anxious to get back to your home and your things," Tara said, repeating his word choices to try and reassure him, to show him they were on the same wavelength. "If you answer my questions, we can talk about taking you back. Is that a good deal?"

He grunted. "No. I want to go back now."

Tara tried a different tack, leaning back further in her chair. "You don't like being here, do you?" She knew most people didn't like to be in the Sheriff's station, especially not in the position of being interviewed, but this seemed to be more than that.

"I want to be alone," he said, shifting as far away from her as he could with his hands cuffed to a bar under the table. "I want to go away and be alone with the trees."

"You can be alone," Tara replied. "Tell me about the girls that go missing up in the woods."

There was no response.

Tara bit her lip. Why wasn't it working? She'd been sympathetic, mirroring his words, acknowledging his struggles. This was exactly how she had managed to get through to Miley Piper. Why wasn't it working with him? She needed to try a different tactic, maybe, but she didn't think that going all-in like she did with other criminals would work. It seemed like he was the kind of person that would just get scared off by harsh or loud words.

"Have you seen any girls up near your cave?" she tried.

He looked away into the far corner of the room, so she was looking at the back of his head.

"You want to go home, right?" Tara said. At this, he looked around and raised his eyebrows – she thought so, anyway, since the hair above his forehead moved. "Tell me about the girls."

"Haven't seen any girls," he muttered, looking away again. Tara thought she saw a hint of redness under the matt of his beard where it reached his cheeks. He was… blushing?

Tara paused, observing him for a second. He looked so uncomfortable. She was starting to have an inkling of something, but she couldn't arrange it without it being too obvious.

"Would you like a hot drink?" she asked. "Coffee? Tea?"

He grunted slightly.

"What about some hot soup?"

He turned half back to face her and then gave a curt nod.

Tara got up and went to the door, nipping outside and closing it behind her. "Glenn!" she stage-whispered across the room.

He rushed over. "What's wrong?"

"Nothing's wrong," Tara said. "Go tell Tracy on reception to bring us a cup of hot soup from the machine."

"Tracy?" Glenn frowned. "Is that safe for her?"

"It will be," Tara said. "Trust me – just send her. And fast."

Glenn nodded. As soon as she asked for his trust, she could see it was there. He practically ran out of the room towards reception, doing what she had asked. Tara smiled to herself. With Glenn having her back, things were so much easier.

She headed back into the room and sat down at the table. "Hot soup's coming," she said. "Can we give you anything else while you're here? We have showers on site, and we can arrange to help you shave and cut your hair if you want."

He shook his head. "Don't need it."

Tara eyed him, grateful he wasn't looking back at her because he would have seen the expression on her face. He very much badly needed it. The smell that rolled off him even from here was largely composed of woody smells – like moss and wet wood and pine needles – but under that was a hefty dose of human body odor. Then again, he didn't seem to be much bothered by it.

"Well, if you change your mind," she said. "How about some warmer clothes?"

He shook his head stubbornly.

Alright, Tara thought. There wasn't much else to do but wait.

She was building up a mental profile of the man in front of her. He was shy, wanted to be away from other humans. He wanted to be out there in nature. Sanitation wasn't an issue for him, and neither was the state of his clothes – apparently he was warm enough.

"Can you tell me what you were doing two nights ago?" she asked. That was a simple enough question. That was something he might be able to answer.

"No," he said.

Tara breathed for a moment, trying not to yell. "If you don't talk to us, then I'm not going to be able to let you go," she said, calmly. More calmly than she felt.

"I can't tell you what I was doing," he said. "I don't keep track."

Tara considered that for a moment. It sounded like the truth. "Do you have a routine that you normally follow?" she asked.

His eyes slid to the other side. "Don't want to tell you."

"You won't get in trouble for telling me," she said.

He paused. "Just have things to do," he said. "Check traps, lay more. Cook dinner. Eat. Clean. Sleep."

Tara nodded. It sounded plausible. A man living out in the forest would have things he needed to take care of in order to survive. Finding food was important.

"Why do you wear dog tags around your neck?" she asked, nodding to the chain that was only just visible around his neck, hidden again behind his clothes. That was the big question. The smoking gun, almost. If he couldn't explain the tags…

"Served," he grunted.

Tara wet her lip carefully, trying to figure out where to take the next question, how to get details from him. "Iraq?" she asked.

He looked down at the floor. "Camp Fallujah," he said. His voice was raw and contained multitudes of hurt. Trauma. Something that might have caused him to shun human company and prefer to live alone in the woods.

She was convinced, now. All she needed was one more thing to prove it to her.

There was a swift knock at the door and it opened after a tiny pause, without time for Tara to actually invite the person to come in. It revealed Tracy, the station's receptionist, on the other side.

Tracy was a big personality, which was why she was great at working reception. She wore low-cut blouses that showed off her ample chest, squeezing down over her waist in a size that was maybe not quite the right one for her body, often coupled with short skirts. Braddock didn't pick her up on it since she spent most of her time behind the desk anyway and therefore no one but those who worked in the office would see it, but it was an overwhelming look for those who didn't know her.

And the second he saw her, the mountain man blushed bright red and turned to face the other wall.

He didn't relax until Tracy left the room, the hot soup remaining behind on the table – and that was all Tara needed to see.

This man wasn't a killer. There was no way he would willingly come closer to any other humans who might be trespassing into the areas he roamed, women or men. And when he did come across a woman, he seemed barely able to handle it. Tara was sure she was only a partial exception because of the fact that she had already arrested him, giving him time to get used to her.

He couldn't have approached anyone else. He couldn't have come far enough into populated areas to abduct anyone – especially not Rosalyn Clement, who had been taken from her home in the middle of town. He just wouldn't have been able to bear it. And when he was confronted with something he didn't like, he didn't react with violence – he just tried to get away as quickly as he could. That was why he had pushed her over in the cave, so he could get to the exit.

She watched as he reached for his soup and then adjusted, having to switch his hands around a few times to get a good grip on the warm cup before bringing it to his mouth. His hands were shaking. His sleeve rode up as he brought the soup to his mouth, and then Tara saw what she hadn't before. His wrists.

His wrists and lower arms were scarred with what looked like burns, the skin tight and twisted, and his hands shook so much he had to put the soup down and steady himself before trying again.

There was no way he had the strength to abduct a healthy young woman like Rosalyn or Miley. He was injured. Tara guessed ongoing nerve damage of some kind, maybe a bomb blast while he was on his tour.

He couldn't hurt anyone – not truly.

"Enjoy your soup," she said, getting up. She came closer to him and unlocked his handcuffs; he cringed away from her and sprang up from the seat as soon as she was done, getting further away from her. Tara turned deliberately and left the room, pausing only at the doorway to make sure he was fine. He was apparently waiting for her to go before he would return to the table. "You can leave when you're done. And if you want, one of us will drive you back to where you were. You just come see us if you want that. You don't have to say anything."

She left the door half-ajar, closed enough that he could retain some privacy but clearly unlocked.

"You're letting him go," Sheriff Braddock said, emerging from the neighboring room into the corridor. It was a statement, not a question.

"He's no killer," Tara said. "And he's not harming anyone, living out there."

"Except himself," the Sheriff grunted.

"Maybe," Tara murmured, glancing back at the door. "But we've already disrupted his life enough. I don't want to charge him for living in the cave. At least this way, we know he's out there."

"Frankly, I don't have time to argue with you, so if you're convinced he's harmless, so be it," Braddock said. "I agree he's not a killer, and that's enough. Our first priority right now is getting Rosalyn Clement back, because she's still out there somewhere."

Tara nodded. She put a hand to her mouth, stifling a reluctant yawn as she checked the time on the clock above the door. It was nearly midnight. Not only would she normally have clocked off by now, but she would have been home in bed, asleep. Wyatt wasn't exactly known for its rock and roll lifestyle.

But now was no time for rest. Not with Rosalyn still missing, and potentially still alive – for now.

“We have until dawn,” Glenn said, his voice dry and tight, as if he was worried by the deadline.

“By dawn?” Tara asked, looking back at the Sheriff wildly. Had she missed something? Was the killer getting in contact to deliver ultimatums?

“That’s when the state department are insisting on taking over,” Braddock said. “If we don’t solve this by dawn, it’s out of our hands.”

CHAPTER TWENTY ONE

"Sit down."

Tara bridled at the instruction. Every single second of wasted time right now was ticking by in her head, creating a tally far too high. But Sheriff Braddock was still her boss, and she still wanted to obey him in the end. She sat, literally having to bite her tongue to keep herself from arguing.

"Look," Braddock said, gesturing to the coffee in her hands. "You need a break. I need a break. Glenn needs a break. If we keep pushing on without any results and we don't rest, we're going to burn out long before dawn."

Tara stared down into the black liquid, wishing it would give her some inspiration. At least the smell alone was doing something for how exhausted she felt. The bleariness around her eyes felt like it lifted some as she took a gulp. "I don't like doing nothing," she said.

"You aren't doing nothing. You're checking in with your mentor." Braddock gave her a steely yet knowing look. "That's what you do when you're stuck, you know. Or it should be. You check in with your wise old mentor and see if he can think of anything that you haven't yet."

"But in this case, my mentor is working alongside me already and would have told me if he had any ideas," Tara said drily. She sighed. "We're getting nowhere. The state police are going to take it. It's been two hours since we let our last suspect go, and we haven't managed to scare up any new leads at all."

"Which means we still have hours to go," Braddock said. He sipped at his own coffee. "As you frequently remind me, Tara, I'm an old man. I've been around for a long time. And you know I've always told you, I've never seen someone with the same raw potential for this work that you have. You're primed and you're ready. You have more reason to care about the work than most. That all works in your favor. Let's use it."

Tara sighed again. "I know you always say that, but I just don't know what that means."

"It means you're going to be a Sheriff yourself one day not too far into the future, and you're going to be a damn better Sheriff than Jessy Strong ever could be," he said, giving her a tiny smirk when she perked up at the mention of her older sister. "You're going to be such a good Sheriff we're going to be fighting off the feds with a stick to stop them from poaching you. You've just got to cut your teeth on cases like this. You have the tools; you have the training. Just put them to work."

"Why don't you do that and solve the case?" Tara couldn't help herself from retorting. He was putting her under so much pressure, and she wasn't even sure she could take it. She wasn't sure she could do it.

"Because," Braddock said seriously, sipping from his cup then putting it down to look right into her eyes. "I'm not as good at this as you are."

Tara almost spluttered her coffee back into the cup. She swallowed carefully. The way he looked at her, she almost began to think…

She almost began to think he might be right.

It was hard to waver in the face of his conviction.

"I still don't know where to turn," she said. "I feel like we've looked into the records of every single local resident at this point. None of those with criminal histories own cabins except the Westons, and we've already cleared Tim."

"Then our killer must not have a criminal record," Sheriff Braddock stated simply.

Tara thought about that for a moment. Maybe it was the juxtaposition of the idea of the killer having passed as innocent with the former presence of their mountain man, but…

She felt like she was getting an idea.

"If you were a killer for a long time," she said, slowly, trying to follow the train of thought. "Then you would know it was really important to lay low. To make sure that people didn't pay too much attention to you – or your cabin. You wouldn't talk about it at the bar or invite friends over. You wouldn't rent it out to tourists. You wouldn't even let people know you had it unless it was unavoidable."

Sheriff Braddock raised an eyebrow, then pointed towards the door out of the breakroom. "Let's walk and talk," he suggested.

Tara took her coffee with her, standing up mostly on autopilot as she walked back towards her desk. "We were probably on the right track with our mountain man, even if we didn't find the right person," she said. "Someone who lives out there, on the outskirts of society. Maybe even off the grid, like he does. If you're off the grid, you can't be traced."

"What's this?" Glenn asked, getting up as they wandered towards him, clearly sensing they were discussing the case.

"The killer," Tara said. "He's never been caught. All of the people we've been looking at, our suspects – we've been trying to find people who have a criminal past. But our killer is successful for exactly the opposite reason. He never gets caught. He's never been in trouble. When you regularly kill people at your cabin, you don't want to give the Sheriff's department or anyone else a reason to sniff around. You don't steal. You don't attack people in town. You don't get into bar fights. You don't so much as drive around with one of your headlights out. It's too much of a risk."

"That makes sense," Glenn nodded thoughtfully. "Usually I would say most criminals start small, get caught a few times, and work their way up, and they aren't always the smartest sort. But if this guy has gone so long without getting caught, I guess he must be smart."

"Sharp," Tara said. "He doesn't have to be well-educated, exactly, but he's sharp. Maybe he teaches himself a lot of things. Reads a lot. Someone who keeps themselves to themselves, educates themselves, has their own particular ways. That would fit with what Miley said, wouldn't it? Someone who has a little awkwardness about them because they don't come into town often."

"Maybe we're looking for someone who lives outside of town," Glenn suggested. "Someone who lives in the cabin and doesn't come down here often."

"There are plenty of people who live out there in the cabins by the lakes or even further into the woods," the Sheriff pointed out.

"But he won't be right there on the main stretch," Tara said. She strode over to the map on the wall. It was an aerial view of the county, printed from online resources and cropped at the county lines. She honed in on the area between the biggest lake, where Miley had run screaming, and the mountain. There was a large stretch of forest that contained the smaller lakes, some smaller hills and cave systems, and a lot of cabins.

But the area of land that both contained cabins but wasn't right on the very edge of a lake was smaller. Take out a couple of areas that had been developed by cynical companies who made hamlets out of the cabins, knowing that people didn't really want to be as isolated as they claimed, as well as the largest road and any cabins that were set just off it…

The catchment area was now much smaller.

"Here," Tara said, circling a large area of woodland with her finger. "He lives somewhere in here. North of the lake, south of the smaller lake systems, and away from the road."

Sheriff Braddock squinted at the map, the tiny gray squares that stood for the roofs of cabins. Some of them wouldn't even be visible on an aerial map, covered by the branches of the trees above them. "There must only be ten or twelve cabins up there." Behind her, she sensed Glenn moving away.

"We have people going door to door in this area, right?" Tara asked, pointing to the smaller lakes.

"Yes," Braddock nodded. "All the deputies we could spare from guarding the lakeside gravesites."

"Then if I'm wrong, we're covered. Who lives up there?"

"I'm pulling the records now," Glenn called over from his desk.

"These ones are rentals," Sheriff Braddock said, pointing to three of them. "They have guests a lot of the year. If you're right and he's keeping attention away from himself, he wouldn't even risk it when the tourist season is in full swing."

"No rentals," Tara agreed.

"We've got a property up there registered to – oh," Glenn said.

"To who?" Tara asked, turning around to stare at him.

"To Roger Bryant," he said. "Isn't that Deputy Bryant's dad?"

"What about my dad?" Bryant called from the other side of the room. He was still sitting by the phones. He was apparently experiencing a lull because he was listening in on everything.

"Nothing," Glenn said hurriedly. "He just lives in a cabin up where we think the killer might be."

"He doesn't live there," Bryant said. "Just uses it for hunting. Who else are you looking into?"

"Uh, let's see," Glenn said slowly. "I guess his nearest neighbor is Annie Cordell."

Bryant snorted. "Annie doesn't go near the place. Aric lives there."

"Aric Cordell," Tara repeated, thinking. She felt like she knew the name.

"He's the guy who only comes into town once a week or so," Bryant supplied. "You've probably seen him or even spoken to him, but you won't see him every day. He's pretty tall, white hair – it's been white for as long as I've known him, but he's only in his forties or so."

"Always wears plaid," Tara said, her brain beginning to supply the gaps. "Blue or red, always pretty faded. Yeah. I think he's been living up there for as long as I've been alive."

"That tracks," Bryant nodded. "Dad says he keeps to himself, pretty much. Doesn't want to spend time with his neighbors or whatever. He's polite enough, but whenever Dad would invite him around for cards or a drink, he would come up with some excuse – but he lives on his own and works on the land, so it's not like he's got a lot on his busy social calendar."

"Can your Dad see him from his cabin?" Tara asked. Her mind was starting to race. A man who kept to himself. Who didn't come into town often, but was polite and quiet when he did. Someone who never raised any eyebrows, except for the fact that he wasn't as social as others. Someone who never got involved in the community. Never drew attention to themselves.

"No, it's too far," Bryant said. "I mean, they may look like neighbors on the map, but it's not like that out there. The forest is pretty thick, and it's a long, trailing road to get to the next property. You could probably get there on foot, but the undergrowth and the branches are thick, and you'd get all scratched up. So it's not an easy thing to just drop in and visit a neighbor. Actually, I don't think I've ever seen the inside of that cabin, not even when I was a boy and I used to go around with my Dad. Aric moved in there when he was a teenager or something I think, right after he left school."

"Bryant," Tara said, trying to keep her tone as even as possible. "Do you realize that what you just said perfectly fits with the location that Miley must have run from?"

Bryant looked at her with wide eyes. "Uh," he said.

"And did you not think that with this lovely bit of local knowledge you have, you might have brought up the fact that you know a loner who lives in the forest on his own and has always been a bit strange when we were looking for a potential killer?" Tara asked, seething slightly. Behind her, Sheriff Braddock put a hand on her shoulder – a warning to calm down.

"Well – it wouldn't be him, though," Bryant said dumbly. "I *know* him."

"You can't rule people out on the basis of knowing them, Bryant!" Tara exploded, burying her face in her hands in frustration for a moment. "Right, before we do anything else – does anyone know anyone other than Aric Cordell who fits the profile of someone living in a cabin up north of the lake, who keeps to themselves and lives alone, who doesn't engage in the community much and doesn't like to draw attention to themselves?"

Glenn and Bryant both gave her blank looks. She didn't feel the need to turn and look at Sheriff Braddock, knowing that he was the last person she needed to worry about ignoring an obvious potential suspect.

"Okay," she said. "Then we're driving up to those cabins right now. Glenn, let's go."

"Wait," Glenn said, his brow furrowing lightly. "Just because he doesn't come into town much?"

"He fits our profile perfectly," Tara said, impatient to go and unable to believe Glenn was forcing her to stand still and explain in detail at this pivotal moment. "He's never drawn attention to himself, never got a criminal record. He doesn't even own the cabin, which explains why we haven't seen his name until now. He's a local and has been for his whole life, which means he knows the area very well – especially the area around the lakes and in the forest, because he spends more time in nature than with people. In fact, he'd be exactly the kind of person who would know what time to go to the lakeshore to avoid being seen by anyone because no one is around at that time. If there's such a huge gap between the cabins out there, it's likely that no one would hear any disturbances up at his place."

"He was a bit weird when he was at school," Bryant said thoughtfully. Tara glared daggers at him. "My Dad always had this joke about him enjoying the dissection lessons a bit too much."

"Bryant," Tara said. "I suggest you look for a new line of work before you become a murder victim yourself."

"Alright, alright," Sheriff Braddock interrupted. "There's no need for that kind of language. And you don't have hiring and firing decisions yet, Deputy Sheriff Strong." The use of her title had the intended effect – putting Tara back in her box.

"He's normal now," Bryant muttered grumpily. "Liking dissection could just mean you're a natural scientist. He's just quiet."

Tara turned on her heel and started to walk out, done with the delays. "I'm going to bring him in," she announced. "Whether I have to do it alone or not."

"You're not going alone," Glenn said hurriedly, and she heard his feet rushing after her. "I believe you."

"I'll take Bryant and circle around the area," Sheriff Braddock said. "We'll take a few positions around the back of the cabin, to the northwest and northeast, to cover us in case he tries to run. Tara and Glenn, you go in the front."

Even with the agreement now, Tara didn't wait for them to catch up with her or slow to help them plan. All she could think about was Rosalyn Clement – alone, scared, having spent almost a full night with her abductor. Maybe he hadn't told her yet that he was going to kill her.

But maybe he had.

She didn't pause when she reached the car, getting behind the wheel and starting it, leaving Glenn to run the last bit of the distance to get into the passenger side before she pulled away without him.

"Let's go save Rosalyn," she said, and when she caught his grim nod of determination as she turned to back out of the parking space, she knew that Glenn had her back.

CHAPTER TWENTY TWO

"He drives a pickup truck," Tara whispered. Glenn, who was standing beside her, nodded. He shivered slightly. They'd left the car behind a few minutes ago, not wanting the headlights or the sound of the engine to give them away, and the night air was cold now.

"It's not purple, is it?" he asked. "It looks darker than that."

"It's faded," she said, keeping her voice to a whisper as Glenn stayed by her side. "The paintwork must be old. Bleached by the sun. Looks like it was black once."

Tara held back, examining the property from the tree line. The cabin was small, but big enough to house a life so long as it was lived alone. It wasn't a temporary structure, by any means – it had been built sturdy and strong and then improved over generations, with double-glazed windows put in and outdoor amenities added. The wooden walls were thick and reinforced with modern techniques, so the inhabitant was not at risk of feeling the cold through cracks in the structure.

"It looks…" Glenn shook his head with wonder. "I mean, if it was full blazing sun and you were getting those refractions off it – it could… almost look purple?"

One of the smaller lakes was not far away, as the crow flew, but the river that fed it burbled by close enough that Tara could hear the water. She remembered what Miley Piper had said and closed her eyes for a moment, trying to imagine what this place sounded like without being able to see it. It wasn't hard to imagine. The night was still dark around them. It was only because her eyes had adjusted well and the moon was still out strong that she could make out much about the cabin at all.

Tara looked over the cabin again, checking it for any signs of life. It was dark there. Not a single light turned on. They were going to have to wake up the resident sooner or later in order to get inside. She decided to take the risk of alerting him to their presence early to check out the truck. Flicking her flashlight on, she stepped forward, running the beam of light over it.

"Let's go wake him up," Tara said. "Be ready for a chase, just in case. And we can't let him close the door on us, no matter what."

"Agreed," Glenn said. "If he tries to lock us out, we have to assume he's planning to kill her."

"Then we take no risks," Tara said. She reached down and checked the position of her gun in her holster. She didn't want to knock on the door with it in her hand and provoke him, but she needed to be ready to draw and fire quickly if it came to it.

She took a breath. The air was cold and laced with the scent of pine, with a hint of moonlight. Her breath came out as a fine mist. The moment seemed to slow down and crystallize.

Tara walked toward the door of the cabin and knocked heavily, loud enough that she hoped it would wake anyone up. "Open up! Sheriff's department," she yelled out. A bird overhead startled and took flight. She didn't look up to see it, but its wings sounded heavy and wide.

There was a scurry of movement inside the cabin immediately. The property was small enough that it wasn't possible to hide; when a light flickered on at the far end of the ground floor, Tara saw it spilling out from the front door. She heard the footsteps making their way across the whole cabin, right up to the door.

The door handle turned, and she braced herself, all of her fear flying to one side as she compartmentalized, focusing on what needed to be done. The door opened just a crack, just enough for Aric Cordell to put his body into the gap and fill it, leaving them no room to enter and no way to look past him.

"Hello?" he said, his voice a little bleary. His white hair – white, not gray – was mussed, as if he had just woken up. Despite the color on top of his head, he looked fit and healthy, his body strong from working outdoors and his skin tanned.

"Aric Cordell," Tara said, stating his name rather than asking him. "I'm Deputy Sheriff Tara Strong, and this is Deputy Grayson."

Aric nodded, folding his arms over his chest as if to ward off the chill. Either his pajamas were plaid, or he slept in his day-clothes – or he hadn't been in bed at all. "I've seen you around town," he nodded.

"We need to come in and speak with you," Tara said, getting right to the point. She needed to get inside, and she was prepared to insist aggressively if needed.

"Uh," he said, glancing behind himself. "Look, the place is a mess. It's the middle of the night. Can't you come back in the morning?"

"No," Tara said. "I'm afraid this is very urgent. It's a safety matter. If we could?" She pointed toward the inside of the cabin, reaching for the door at the same time.

"Uh, it's," Cordell said, trying to stop her – but Tara had already pushed the door wide open, leaving her looking into the space beyond.

"There's no problem, is there?" Tara asked. "Only it's freezing cold out here, so I'd quite like to get inside as quickly as possible."

"Um, sure," he said, stepping to one side. "Sure. Come in."

Tara was quick to take the opportunity, moving before he could change his mind. She was bold, pushing right through the door and stepping past him, not allowing herself to think about the fact that she was putting herself into close quarters with a man who she believed to be a serial killer.

But then again, since he'd let her in so easily, could it really be the case? Wouldn't the real killer argue with her and ask her not to come in?

She looked around the cabin, seeing a little mess but not something that you would really be so embarrassed about. "Do you mind if we look around?" she asked, as Cordell closed the door behind Glenn.

"Uh," Cordell said, then shrugged helplessly, his hands going out to the sides. "Sure, I guess." He sounded reluctant, but also like he was giving in since they were already inside anyway.

"Thanks," Tara said, flashing him an insincere smile. "This is a public safety issue, as I mentioned."

"Uh, yeah, it must be," Cordell said. He trailed after her as she walked across the living space with keen eyes, peering around the corners and into every gap between the furniture. There was no telling what clues there might be – a high heel here, a bowl full of marked dog tags there. "For you to come out at this hour of the night and wake folks up in their beds."

"We take this matter very seriously," Tara said with another tight smile. She knew he was fishing, trying to ask questions about what they were doing, but she wasn't going to give him anything. He was going to have to ask outright, and even then she would evade.

There was a nagging voice in the back of her head that kept insisting: Why is he so calm? Why doesn't he stop us from coming in or looking around? Why isn't he trying to run, or else trying to stop us from looking around?

Why doesn't this feel like the home of a killer?

Glenn disappeared into the bathroom, then reemerged and entered the bedroom. It was the only other room in the place, and divided from everything by the use of a curtain, not a door. He quickly exited the room and stood again next to Tara, giving a quick shake of his head.

But Tara wasn't done yet. She turned and pointed toward a square shape on the floor, an outline that was only just visible in the wooden boards and half-hidden under a rug. A trap door.

"Where does that go?" Tara asked.

"Well," Cordell said, and then stopped.

"Well?" Tara prompted. "An underground storage space, maybe?"

"There's a basement," he said reluctantly.

"Open it, please, and then step back," Tara said.

Cordell swallowed, but he moved over toward it. There was a keyhole in the wood and he fitted a key to it from his pocket, unlocking and then opening the door. It swung upwards, revealing a black hole into a dark space with a ladder leading downwards. He stepped back obediently, waiting silently beside it. There wasn't much room for him to go – with the door open, the three of them standing there, and the meager furniture he had, they would have to shuffle around one another to get anywhere.

"Does it have a light?" Tara asked.

Cordell nodded. "Cord's inside, as you go down the ladder. 'Bout halfway."

Tara eyed the hole uncertainly. She'd seen enough horror movies, a Friday night tradition that she liked to unwind with. She had the distinct feeling that if both she and Glenn went down there, they would find themselves locked in. She wasn't sure she wanted to be down there *with* Cordell, either, if there was a possibility of something down there being dangerous.

But what was the alternative? They couldn't all stand up here looking into a black pit and expecting something to come up.

"Glenn," Tara said. "You stay up here. I'll go down and take a look." She hoped the words sounded calm enough to Cordell, but tense enough to Glenn. His job was to stay upstairs and guard Cordell, and also guard the only way back up out of the basement to be sure that she couldn't be trapped down there.

Her job was to go down there and check it out.

Oh, God.

Tara felt her heart leaping up into her mouth as she thought of going down there. Down into darkness. Down with no clue what was waiting for her. What was she about to walk into? A torture dungeon where Rosalyn Clement was strung up? A whole bunch of bodies waiting to be buried by the lake, kept on ice until then?

An accomplice waiting to tie her up and put her in one of the rooms that Miley Piper had described, all on her own?

She swallowed down her fear, knowing that she had no choice.

Tara put one foot on the ladder and then the other, moving down a step and glancing back at Glenn as she did so.

She tried not to think that this might be the last time she would ever see him, and took another few steps down into the pitch black.

She reached out to the side, groping blindingly, until her fingers connected with a cord. She pulled it and the basement flooded with light, filling her with relief at the same time. There was, at first glance, nothing terrifying down here after all.

Tara climbed all the way to the bottom and looked up. She knew in her head that it wasn't a long way, but somehow, Glenn and Cordell looked really far out of her reach. The kind of distance away that if Cordell decided to spring forward and close the door and take Glenn out, she wouldn't be able to get back up there in time.

She needed to just search the basement as quickly as possible. Get back up there before anything could go wrong.

Tara cast around quickly. The basement was what you would expect from someone who lived out in the woods full-time. There was a lot of hunting and camping gear, including folded-up tarps, a tent in a bag, camouflage clothing, and netting that might be used to cover a hide. There were no guns, which made Tara's heart thud in her chest when she considered that any Cordell had would be up there with him.

Turning to the other side of the basement, Tara walked across to a rack of wine that was covered in a coating of dust, a bookcase that was stacked with dried and tinned goods instead of books, and a chest freezer.

A chest freezer…

Okay, now this was one she was absolutely sure she had seen in all the horror movies, not to mention every serious crime thriller ever. If he was the killer, there was a body in that freezer. There was no question in Tara's mind.

She stepped closer to it, her hand shaking as she reached out towards the catch. She froze when she noticed a reddish-brown stain on the side of the freezer right by the catch, as though blood had dripped out while he was putting the body in. She swallowed hard. They still didn't know how he killed them.

She lifted the latch and then used both hands to push the lid up into the air, letting it settle back against the wall.

What was that…? She turned over one of the packets on top, and…

Frozen berry mix.

It was a frozen berry mix, packaged up for easy use in smoothie makers. It looked like it had been opened and sealed up again. That was what the trail of red was – he'd spilled some last time he took it out.

Tara turned over the other items at the top of the freezer and dusted off a few labels. There was frozen meat, frozen vegetables, ice cream. All the kinds of things that you might need if you didn't like going into town often and wanted to be able to survive a snow-in or some other kind of natural disaster.

Everything down here looked perfectly normal.

And again, Tara was reminded. He'd let them in. He'd shown her the way down and allowed her to look around his basement without complaint. What had she really been expecting to find? Aric Cordell was acting like a man who had nothing to hide, except for the fact that he didn't particularly like being woken up in the middle of the night by strangers.

She'd got it wrong. Again. Gone flying off the handle and investigated the first name that came up instead of checking out the other possibilities – again. She had dragged the rest of the department's available hands along with her. Woken up a local resident in the middle of the night for no reason.

And the worst part was, all of that meant that there were less people looking for Rosalyn Clement in the right places, and the missing girl was going to die while Tara wasted everyone's time.

Tara took one last look around the rectangular space of the basement and then pressed her hand against her forehead, realizing she was going to have to climb back up the stairs and admit her mistake. She was going to have to apologize. Not just to Aric, but to Glenn and the others too.

And they still weren't any closer to finding their missing girl.

Tara put her hands on the bottom of the ladder and began to climb, hoping that they would buy the fact that her cheeks were red from the exertion rather than the total humiliation of getting it this badly wrong.

"Alright," she said, as she reached the top. Glenn and Cordell were right where she had left them – Glenn with his hands on his hips as if he was trying to make himself wider and more intimidating, and Cordell hunched over with his arms crossed over his chest. "Thank you, Mr. Cordell. We've seen everything we need to, here."

"Great," he said. "Uh, you need anything else?"

"No, that'll do it," Tara said. She glanced around the square living space. There was still nothing there, just like there never had been. "Thank you for giving us your time. I appreciate this must have been very inconvenient for you. I can only apologize for waking you at this hour, but I assure you, the seriousness of the case did warrant it."

"I understand," Cordell said, nodding tightly. "You guys gotta do your duty and all that."

"Right," Glenn nodded, clapping him on the shoulder in a friendly way. "We'll get out of your way and let you get back to bed."

Tara was heading for the door, ready to leave and tell Sheriff Braddock the bad news. She crossed the space –

And a shiver ran down the back of her neck.

Something had been bubbling away in the back of her mind, slowly coming back up, two things marinating and creating something new.

Something wasn't right here. Something wasn't right about the footprint of the cabin.

Down there in the basement, the space had been rectangular. The whole ceiling was wood slats, supported by beams, which meant she could see full well that the whole space above here was covered by the cabin itself. But the space they were standing in, together with the bedroom and bathroom she could see through the open doors – it was square.

Tara turned left and then right, wondering. Was it possible that the living space of the cabin was larger than the basement? Covered more space? But…

Down there it had seemed so large.

"Anyway, thanks," she said, and walked outside, still not quite sure what to make of what she had seen.

"What?" Glenn muttered low, the second that the door closed behind them. He must have sensed that Tara wasn't quite convinced.

Tara turned and looked at the cabin. She walked around it in a half-circuit.

"It's rectangular," she said.

"So?" Glenn whispered, his voice loud in the relative quiet of the night.

"So, inside it was square," Tara hissed back. "And this wall – there's no windows."

Glenn stared at it for a moment. "That's in the back of the bedroom."

"There's a hidden room," Tara said, with absolute conviction. She wasn't quite sure how this all fit together with Miley's description of a room with a window – maybe he'd kept her in his own bedroom for some reason, but they could figure out all of that later. For now, she had a feeling in her gut that told her with absolute certainty that there was a hidden space in that room, and that was where they would find Rosalyn Clement. "Go get Sheriff Braddock."

"What are you going to do?" Glenn asked.

"I'm going back in," Tara said, and walked back toward the door with determination.

CHAPTER TWENTY THREE

Tara knocked on the door loudly, plastering a false bright smile over her face when Cordell cracked it open. "Hey!" she said. "Sorry – silly me. I put my radio down somewhere in the basement and I didn't pick it up again on the way out. Sorry about this – I'll just go right down and grab it." She was babbling, talking too fast in her nervousness.

"Wait there," Cordell said. "I'll grab it for you."

"Oh, that's very kind, but really," Tara said, quickly pushing the door open again as she had before. "I don't want to put you out. I'll just scamper on down that ladder and back up again, and then I'll be out of your hair." Scamper? She sounded like an idiot. He was going to notice and say something. He was going to see that she was lying to get inside. He would slam the door – or attack her – or…

"Right," he sighed. He apparently saw that he wasn't going to be able to stop her from entering. She had a foot inside the door anyway, and he ended up having to step back or get pushed out of the way as she blustered through.

Tara didn't go right for the basement door, which was already closed again. She paused as if pretending she wasn't sure she should go right on in, then gestured to it. "Oh, did you lock it already?"

"Yeah," Cordell grunted. He pulled the key out of his pocket and bent down to fit it in the lock.

Tara didn't stay to watch him do it. It had taken him a few seconds last time, and now that she was inside, he couldn't stop her. She took advantage of his turned back and dashed sideways into the bedroom, her eyes searching. There had to be a way to get into that room. A way that he controlled. She looked at the ground. There was a scuff mark on the wood – a semi-circular scrape where something had passed over that part of the floorboards over and over. Right in front of a standalone closet that filled the space almost all the way to the ceiling.

"What are you doing?" Cordell asked.

Tara turned to find him behind her, filling the doorframe in the same way. Blocking her exit entirely. But it didn't matter. She had to get into that room.

She had to get to Rosalyn Clement.

Tara turned away from him again and rushed toward the closet, grabbing, and pushing the wood. It was heavy – not too heavy to move. It began to shift immediately, clearly well-greased from having moved this way so many times.

"Get away from there," Cordell snapped. And there he was. The real Aric Cordell. Tara glanced over her shoulder and saw a snarl on his face, distorting his mouth, angry fire flashing out of his eyes. There was no more calm and accommodating citizen. No longer a loner who just wanted to get back to sleep.

He was angry with her, and a vein stood out in his neck as Tara pushed the closet the rest of the way to the wall, keeping her eyes locked with his.

She didn't need to turn around to see what she had found. There was a cold metal door handle pressing into her back when she stepped backwards. She could feel it through the fabric of her uniform. The secret room was back there. She'd found it.

She must have found Rosalyn, too.

"You're sticking your nose into something you don't understand," Aric Cordell snarled, and then he rushed towards her.

Tara put up her hands in front of herself, the only thing she could think of to do in the time she had, and she braced herself for the impact. She managed to step aside, as if she could walk away from him and get out of there, but all that happened was that when he slammed her into the wall she at least didn't have the door handle in her kidneys. Tara gasped for breath, her body leaning forward automatically to get away from the pain, and before she could react again, Cordell had her up against the wall once more by her throat.

"You can't ruin this," he hissed right into her face, his eyes wide and straining, bloodshot around the edges. "You can't take her from me."

Tara wanted to speak, to say something cool, to tell him that she wasn't his to be taken from in the first place. But when she opened her mouth, nothing came out but a gasp for air. She tried to breathe in and nothing happened, his arm crushed up against her windpipe and not letting any oxygen through. She couldn't breathe.

She couldn't breathe.

Tara tugged at his arm, struggled, and fought, but he was far stronger. He was enraged, too, and though she was fighting for her life, it didn't seem to make any difference. He was stronger, and she started to realize she was slipping, black spots appearing in her vision.

There was only one thing she could do. She had one hand free. She had to use it.

She reached down to her own belt, groping along it to her holster, gripping the handle of her gun. She fought to get enough elbow space to draw it, to raise it, lifting it with the last of her strength to point it at his stomach…

"Don't shoot," Aric said, stepping back.

She barely knew what had happened for a moment. She had not pulled the trigger and yet he was gone, the pressure from her neck disappearing. He'd gone voluntarily, feeling the muzzle of her gun pressed against him. For a moment all she did was heave in huge deep breaths, bringing as much of the missing oxygen as she could back into her lungs and her body. Black spots cleared from her vision and she tried to straighten, keeping the gun fixed on him as well as she could. She saw Glenn rush into the room in her peripheral vision, grabbing Cordell just in time as she doubled over to cough, having to drop her gun to aim at the floor as she did so.

When Tara could finally stand up straight and look around, leaning back against the wall for balance, she saw Glenn on the floor beside the bed, sitting on top of Aric Cordell with his hands wrenched behind his back and cuffed together.

She would have been able to shoot him. But she was glad Aric had saved himself instead. Because this way, they could interview him – they could put him on trial. There was a chance they would understand what had happened to all of the girls he had killed and where their bodies were. The families of those who were still missing would be able to get justice.

And Rosalyn Clement…

"Go," Glenn said, catching Tara's eye. His voice was ragged, and his eyes said so much. They said that he had been watching her anxiously to see if she was alright and now understood that she was. They said that he knew her well enough to know that the one thing on her mind was finding their missing girl. They said that he had things under control, that he would keep them under control, and that she could go ahead and do her part.

Tara turned and yanked at the door handle, finding it open. Whether the closet itself had served as enough of a lock to prevent escape, or whether Cordell simply hadn't managed to lock it in time while answering the door, she didn't know – but the door opened, and she rushed into the secret room, her heart in her mouth.

The room was only a few feet wide. There was a single bed, almost more of a prison-style cot than a real bed. Slumped on her side on it was a figure with red hair, wearing a short red dress that hugged her figure. Rosalyn. Tara knew it was Rosalyn.

She was bound hand and foot, her arms behind her back and hitched to her ankles, a configuration of rope that made it almost impossible for her to do anything more than wiggle her fingers and toes – with no chance of escape. She looked up at Tara, raising her head the smallest amount from the bed. Her eyes were wide and wild. Green eyes, even in the dim light coming through the door. Her mouth was bound with a gag.

"Don't worry," Tara gasped, stumbling forward and almost tripping in her haste to holster her gun and get to Rosalyn. "Don't worry. You're safe now. It's over."

She heard Sheriff Braddock and Deputy Bryant's voices out in the cabin as she tugged the ropes undone, allowing Rosalyn to finally move what must have been aching limbs and get up, to try to stand. She was sobbing. She fell on her first attempt, no doubt stiff and sore from the binding. She collapsed against Tara who held her up tightly, finding her own eyes wet as she realized how close both of them had just come to death.

And now it was over.

It was all over.

Except for that one question – about the windows, none of which were broken.

***

Tara blew on the coffee in her cup and then took another sip, wincing slightly as the heat of the liquid singed her tongue. It was worth it, though, for what felt like life-giving worth spreading through her body.

"Are you sure you're alright?" Glenn asked again, for what must have been the seventeenth time already.

"I'm fine," Tara said. She lifted her head, looking out of the windows of the Sheriff's station at the dawn that was just breaking over the horizon. "The doctor said I'm fine. I promise you I'm fine."

"Okay," Glenn nodded, though it was fairly obvious that he was going to ask her if she was alright again in perhaps five or a maximum of ten minutes. "You just looked like you were lost in thought."

"I am lost in thought," Tara said. She took another scalding sip of coffee with a shudder. "I keep thinking about how it just doesn't match up."

"What doesn't match up?" Glenn asked.

"Miley Piper." Tara set the coffee down, then instantly regretted the loss of the warmth from her hands and picked it back up. She wasn't even that cold. Maybe it was a comfort thing. "She told us that she was kept in a normal-sized bedroom. Well, I could maybe buy that she was in the real bedroom instead of the secret room for some reason – though I can't imagine what. But the fact that she said she went through the window… it can't be true. That window was solid as anything, and it definitely hasn't been broken for a long time. There was dust on the inside – dirt and rain marks on the outside. That window wasn't replaced in the last two days – no chance."

"Yeah," Glenn said. He shrugged lightly. "I don't know. Maybe she was held somewhere else. Or maybe she just remembered it wrong because she was in such a state of panic. That can happen, can't it?"

"I guess," Tara said. She didn't feel convinced. Not even remotely.

"It doesn't matter, really, does it?" Glenn asked. "We've got him. We know that Aric Cordell is the killer. We caught him red-handed, literally."

"Right," Tara nodded. She tried to smile, though it felt fake. "You're right. We have him."

She told herself to believe it. She needed to believe it. If he wasn't the right man, then…

"And Rosalyn Clement is safe," Glenn added. "I just heard from the Sheriff. She's been given a clean bill of health at the hospital. She's just in shock, which they say won't last long."

"That's a relief," Tara said. It felt like a physical weight that came off her shoulders. Rosalyn was fine. They'd saved her. They had actually managed to save her life.

"Um, actually," Glenn said. "Sheriff Braddock said that if you're feeling up to it…"

Tara looked up sharply as he trailed off. "What?"

"Are you sure you're alright?" Glenn asked. He grimaced, looking at her neck. "Your throat…"

"I'm fine," Tara insisted. "See? My voice isn't even scratchy anymore. I'm fine. It was only for a few seconds, really – less than a minute. I promise you I'm fine, Glenn."

"He said that if you're fine, we can start Cordell's formal interview," Glenn said, finally giving her the reason he'd come to sit with her in the first place.

How many minutes had passed of wasted time that they could already have been in there, talking to him?

"He doesn't want us to wait for him?" Tara asked, her eyes wide with surprise.

"No, he's overseeing the search of the cabin," Glenn said. "He doesn't know how long it will take and he wants us to get on with the interviewing so he can focus on that. It's not like he won't be able to watch the recorded footage back later."

"Right," Tara said. She took one more sip of the coffee, mourned for her poor burned tongue, and then stood up. "Let's go talk to him now."

"Are you -"

"Glenn," Tara said evenly. "I love being partnered with you, I really do – but I swear to God, if you ask me if I'm alright one more time, I will ask the Sheriff to partner me up with Deputy Bryant from now on."

Glenn made an offended noise. "You wouldn't!"

"Try me and find out," Tara said, casting a look back at him over her shoulder that was half-amusement and half-fire.

He followed her toward the interview room, where Aric Cordell had been waiting in cuffs since they had brought him in. Tara looked through the small window in the door. He was sitting next to a lawyer in a dark suit – someone brought in from a neighboring county on short notice, since they didn't have anyone in Edgar who knew how to represent a murder suspect. The two of them looked, of all things, bored.

"Let's go in," she said, turning to look at Glenn for confirmation. He nodded, though he looked nervous, and Tara went in without another thought. Maybe she should have been nervous, too. But she'd already faced down Aric Cordell once, and she knew that if Glenn hadn't arrived, she could have shot him dead. He didn't scare her. Not now.

Tara sat down in one of the chairs opposite Cordell and his lawyer, and Glenn sat next to her. She looked at Cordell, looked him right in the eye without blinking or flinching. If he thought he was going to get away with this, or weasel out of it, or somehow leave this room without making a full confession, he was wrong.

"Aric Cordell," she said, beginning the conversation. "How many people have you killed?"

He stared back at her, absolutely silent.

"My client has been advised not to offer any answer to your questions," the lawyer said smoothly. "You can consider his answer, in any case, to be 'no comment.'"

Tara tilted her head to one side, looking at Cordell and ignoring the lawyer. She needed to speak directly to him if she was going to get anywhere. The lawyer obviously had full intentions of protecting his client with ironclad silence, but Tara knew that she needed to get through that if they were going to get a confession.

"That doesn't sound very smart," she told Cordell. "We caught you with Rosalyn Clement right there in your cabin. Do you think we'll believe that you had nothing to do with that?"

"My client does wish to offer the correction that the cabin does not belong to him," the lawyer interjected. "The cabin actually belongs to Annie Cordell."

Tara gave Cordell a narrowed-eye look. "You're going to try to put the blame on your own sister? See her go to jail for life for what you did?"

There was no response from either Cordell or the lawyer, who was suddenly very busy going through a stack of papers, reading a few lines on each one and shuffling them.

Tara sighed. "This is a waste of everyone's time," she said. "Do you really want to spend your last days before you go into prison just sitting there silently? You might as well talk to us. Tell us your story. This is your chance to make sure the record is straight."

Silence.

"Alright, I'll do the talking," Tara said. "We know you've been killing them for years. We found your second victim – Ness Griffin was her name. Did you ever know her name? It was seven years ago that you killed her."

She waited. She'd given the wrong information on purpose – it was six years ago that Ness Griffin had been abducted and killed. She wanted to get him annoyed, make him correct her.

"What was your motive?" Glenn spoke up. Tara glanced sideways at him, but it seemed like he'd caught on to what she was doing. "Why did you take these girls and kill them?"

"Did you mean to kill them, or did you take them for some other reason?" Tara asked. "It must get lonely living out in those woods on your own."

"Did you want them to stay with you?" Glenn asked. "Was that it? And when they rejected you, did you kill them then?"

"Because they must have rejected you," Tara said, exchanging a glance with Glenn and then a half-chuckle. She gestured up and down towards Cordell's body and figure. "I mean, look at you. Of course they would reject you."

Nothing. Cordell just stared ahead impassively as if she hadn't even said anything.

"Are you quite done with the personal insults?" the lawyer asked calmly. "My client does have certain rights, you know."

Tara looked at the lawyer and then away, back at Cordell again. "You've been very careful, all these years," she said, trying a different tack. "But it's all over now. Do you understand that? It's over. We've found the bodies by the lake. We've found the dog tags. We know. You may as well tell us everything and save yourself a trial."

Silence.

Tara felt the confidence that had buoyed her into the room beginning to fade. The lawyer had done a good job of preparing his client during the time they'd been waiting to interview him. He was too ready. Too steadfast on what he needed to do in order to be in with the best chance of getting away with it.

But surely he didn't believe that he would get away with it. Not when he'd been caught right there in the cabin with Rosalyn.

"You must know that you're going to go to prison for a very long time, no matter what happens here," Tara said. "There's no jury in the world that would believe you didn't know Rosalyn was there, behind a wall in your own bedroom. There's no jury in the world that would think it wasn't you who took her. And she's going to be able to give a witness statement too – along with your other victim that escaped. She came right to us, you know. She told us everything. Between the two of them, we have enough witness testimony to make sure you never breathe free air again."

Aric Cordell looked her right in the eyes, and she saw something kind of smooth out between them. His forehead was flat, as if he didn't have a worry or care in the world, as if it wasn't even difficult for him to stay quiet.

In that moment, Tara knew she wasn't going to break him – not with the tools she had on hand right now. He clearly didn't mind the fact that he was caught with Rosalyn in the cabin with him. Whatever his lawyer had said to him, he'd made Aric Cordell feel like it wasn't going to be a problem so long as he just stayed quiet.

She needed to find another method of attack.

And as she sat there looking at their killer, she knew exactly who to ask to help her find it.

CHAPTER TWENTY FOUR

Glenn looked doubtfully over at the door to the interview room, then back at Tara. "You want me to what?" he asked.

"I want you to interview him on your own," Tara said again, but it made even less sense the second time.

"I don't think I'm going to make any progress if you can't," Glenn protested.

Tara grinned, which was somehow unsettling. "I don't expect you to, not really," she said. "Just keep chipping away at him. The longer he has to sit there in silence, the more likely it is that he's going to break. Even if you just ask him the same question over and over at thirty-second intervals, let him know that we're not going to break first."

Glenn considered it. He always did everything with Tara. Not only was she his partner, but she was senior to him – which meant that if there was ever a case of something needing to be done solo, she was usually the one to take it on, not him.

But she was looking at him with total confidence, like it wasn't a question. Like she just assumed he would be able to handle it.

"Okay," he said, not wanting to let her down or admit that he was nervous.

"I'll see you later," Tara said, grabbing her cell phone and making towards the door. "If anything comes up, just call me. I'll be back later."

"Right," Glenn said, and then grinned. "I'll call you when he tells me everything."

Tara laughed on the way out of the door, apparently appreciating his joke – or his confidence; Glenn couldn't tell.

But as soon as she was gone, he sank back down into the familiar chair at his desk, not sure exactly how he was going to do this.

He didn't have the same level of experience Tara had, and he was pretty sure he also didn't have the same instinct for interviews. He usually just followed her lead and went with whatever she thought was the best strategy. Not that he'd ever had to interview anyone for a crime this serious before, anyway. How was he supposed to do this?

He stood up from the chair, steeling himself. All he had to do was keep the guy talking, right? It wasn't about actually getting him to confess. That would have been a great result, but it wasn't necessary. Tara just needed him to keep Cordell busy. That, he could do, couldn't he?

Right. Even though he was going to be sitting opposite a serial killer, it was probably going to be fine. Even though the man had probably killed, like, five people. If not more. At least they had all been women.

That they knew of.

Glenn squared his shoulders. He could do this. He was just as good an investigator as anyone in the Sheriff's department. He just needed to –

The phone rang on his desk, and Glenn dropped back into the chair gratefully, grabbing it out of the cradle. "Hello, Sheriff's department, Deputy Grayson speaking."

"Deputy Grayson, I'm calling from the hospital," a female voice on the other side of the line said. "It's regarding our patient – Rosalyn Clement."

"Oh, yes?" Glenn asked. He hoped she was alright. He prayed this wasn't a call in which he found out she'd taken some kind of turn for the worse.

"She has indicated to us that she's ready for an interview," the nurse said. "The Sheriff went on out to look into something at the lake, and he said to call right in to the station there if she was ready."

"Right," Glenn said, realizing this was his opportunity to step up. "Right, thanks! I'll be over there soon."

He hung up, glancing toward the door of the interview room with a modicum of regret. He'd just got his nerve up, too. But Aric Cordell was going to have to wait. Maybe stewing in there with his lawyer would be the best thing for him.

Glenn had someone much better to talk to, and if Tara's tactic was to get more witness testimony to use against Cordell, then Rosalyn Clement could only help. He just wished he could get hold of Tara and call her back here to do it – but she was already gone, and since she'd wanted him to take charge, that was what he was going to do.

***

Glenn gave Rosalyn a breezy, cheerful smile, hoping that it would put her at ease. He hadn't been in the room to see how Tara had approached Miley Piper, but anyway, Rosalyn was giving him a different impression. She didn't look scared. She looked angry.

"Rosalyn," he said. "I'm Deputy Grayson. Do you remember me from last night?"

"I do," she nodded. "You were there when the Deputy Sheriff found me."

"Right," Glenn nodded in confirmation. "The nurses said you were ready to talk to me about what happened to you."

"Yeah, I'm ready," Rosalyn said. "I'm ready to take those sons of bitches down. I'll tell you anything you need to know."

Glenn hesitated, tilting his head at her word choice. "Plural?"

Rosalyn looked back at him. "Well, yeah. Both of them."

Glenn was pretty sure that if his eyes popped open wider, they would have fallen out of his skull. "Wait a second. We only know about one suspect. Who are you talking about?"

"There was the guy you arrested in the cabin," Rosalyn said. "He's the one who abducted me."

"We have him in custody now," Glenn replied. It was good that she was identifying Cordell right off the bat. That would help with the case against him. "But what about the other person you saw?"

"I didn't see them," Rosalyn hesitated. "Actually, I didn't see the man you arrested until the end either, but I heard his voice and I know it was him. And he only talked about the other one."

"What do you mean?" Glenn asked, his brow furrowing. He wasn't getting it, not yet.

"He was telling me all about her," Rosalyn said. "How she helped him out before and she was going to prove herself soon. He said it didn't matter what he told me because I wasn't going to live long enough to tell anyone else. He told me he knew she was going to be able to come through and kill me."

Glenn stared at her, his mind racing.

"Just hold on for a moment," he said, and he turned to walk out of the room. He needed to think this over.

A woman who was an accomplice for Aric Cordell. Someone who had helped him in the past – someone who he believed was on the path to kill again.

Cordell had been very careful over the years. He had managed to space his victims out in such a way that they were never suspected. He was only caught because one of his victims had escaped.

Taking another victim so soon afterwards – it just didn't fit with his usual method. He normally took breaks between his attacks. And the numbers on the dog tags – they didn't work. Two, then seven, and then five?

Something occurred to him, and he turned and went back into the room.

"Rosalyn," he said. "I'm sorry, I just need to ask – did he give you a dog tag?"

"Yeah," Rosalyn said, frowning. "The forensics lady took it off me. It was just a single tag, no chain or anything."

"What number was on it?" Glenn asked. He made a mental note to touch base with Lindsie. She shouldn't have taken a piece of evidence without notifying the other members of the team what was on it – especially not something so pivotal. Surely, she must have known it was significant.

"A ten," Rosalyn said. "Didn't you get it? I asked if I should tell someone else about it, but she said it was fine and she'd share it with everyone."

Glenn frowned. "When did this happen?" he asked.

"Here in the hospital," Rosalyn said. "Not long after I came in. Everyone went out for a minute to let me rest but then she came in and took the tag. I thought it was weird because they had already taken my clothes for samples."

Glenn's mind was racing. Why would Lindsie have come back after taking everything else, then hidden the discovery? She was normally conscientious, good at her job. It didn't fit with what he knew of her.

Unless… it hadn't been Lindsie at all.

"What did she look like?" he asked, his throat suddenly tight.

"I don't know… young," Rosalyn shrugged. "She had red hair."

Glenn stared at her for a beat. Lindsie's hair was dark brown.

He turned on his heel, racing back out of the room. "Thanks," he called over his shoulder. He couldn't stay any longer to be any more polite than that.

There were two killers. Two people involved in the case.

And one of them had been in their hands all along.

Miley Piper wasn't an innocent survivor who had managed to escape.

She was the killer's accomplice.

And Tara had just headed out alone into the wilderness with her.

Glenn grabbed his cell phone out of his pocket as he half-ran through the halls of the hospital, trying not to knock anyone over. He hit dial on Tara's number and put it to his ear, willing it to ring faster.

It rang. Just once. And then, right away, the voicemail message took over.

Glenn cursed under his breath and put on a burst of speed. She was out of the range of signal.

And now the only thing he could do was to race over there and get to her – before something happened that he was never going to forgive himself for.

CHAPTER TWENTY FIVE

Miley was looking out of the window when the car stopped, lost in thought. Lost in her plans.

"Here we are," the Deputy Sheriff said. Tara, her name was.

Miley looked around, jolted out of her inner world and back into reality – or rather, the fake reality she had built up for Tara. She pretended to be nervous, glancing around in all directions and then focusing on the cabin like she was seeing something right out of her nightmares.

"It's alright," Tara said softly. "I'm here with you. And he's not there anymore. We have him in custody. He can't hurt you anymore."

Miley made herself swallow hard and then nod and smile, like she was forcing herself to put on a brave face. Then she turned to get out of the car, which gave her a moment to relax and then recompose her face.

This business of acting the whole time was exhausting. Thankfully, it was going to be over soon. At least, for this time. She would be able to do it more in the future – and she would probably even get used to it. At least, Miley was counting on that.

She wanted to be as helpful to Aric as possible, after all. And if she could lure people in for him instead of him needing to risk himself by taking them, then so much the better.

"What do you think?" Tara asked, watching her as she moved around the front of the car. The sun was up now, but the headlights of the car were still needed to penetrate the gloom of the thick trees. They illuminated the cabin, leaving a Miley-shaped shadow on the wall when she stepped in front of them. "Is this the right place?"

Miley walked up slowly, as if she was trying to rack her brains to remember. She knew it was right, of course. Now she had to decide how to play this.

She had been so careful in leading them astray. She'd told them about the broken window, which was a total fabrication. She had moved the cabin a lot closer to the lake in her telling, so that no one would have thought to look this far from the shore. She had created a bedroom that had nothing to hide, completely opposite to the reality of the hidden room. She'd thought that she would have bought them more time.

This was her backup plan, see. Her get out of jail free card. She couldn't possibly be a suspect if she was a victim. She couldn't be held up over the fact that her fingerprints were in the room if they knew she'd been held in it.

Well, maybe it had been shortsighted to describe a different room if she was going to use that defense. But she had always intended to claim distorted trauma memories from the start.

"I think this is it," she said, letting her voice waver and wobble. "I don't know. I was so scared – I just ran without looking back."

"I understand," Tara soothed, holding out a hand towards her, letting it hover over Miley's back. She really thought she was good at her job, didn't she? It made Miley want to laugh out loud, but that would have given the game away. "Let's go inside and take a look, shall we?"

Miley had expected there to be a guard of some sort outside the cabin – someone making sure that no one trespassed or interfered with the evidence – but the property was unguarded. There was no one else around but the two of them, and tape over the door. What was tape really going to do if someone wanted to go in?

Tara unlocked the door to the cabin with a key she had on her belt, then pushed the door open. She ducked inside first under the tape, holding it up just enough for Miley to duck under it after her. Miley stood up straight in the main room, her eyes darting around keenly.

It hadn't changed since she had left, a little over a week ago. They had made some changes themselves first, taking away every trace of her or the fact that she had called this place home. Or at least, a second home. She came and went as she pleased since that day he had picked her up, three years ago. She was supposed to be his fifth.

The way he always said it – she had ended up being his second in command.

She'd never dreamed, three years ago, that they would end up this way. That she would end up helping him so much, partnering with him, and aiding him in the taking and ending of his girls. There was a thrill in it. A power. And the way he looked at her after it was done…

They'd never spoken about love. She didn't think there was really any romance between them at all. But she held a certainty deep inside her chest that even if she one day married and had children, there would never be anyone who ever looked at her with the same level of worship.

"Did he hold you in here?" Tara asked, gesturing to the bedroom.

Miley stepped through the doorway. *Only at night after a successful one*, she thought. Out loud, she said, "I remember this room. But… but I don't think I was in here. I think I was… through there." She pointed to the half-open entrance to the secret room.

Of course, she had to say she'd been in there now that it had been found. Her fingerprints would be all over the place. They often cleaned up, but they weren't naïve enough to believe that they would be able to get all traces.

Miley's fingers twitched at her side, aching for her normal nervous habit. Turning the dog tag over and over in her hands had been a habit for a long time now. She had almost worn the edges smooth. She loved that tag – that reminder that he had been planning to kill her. There was something darkly beautiful about it. And it was a reminder, too, that instead of extinguishing her life he had recognized her. Seen in her the darkness that was waiting to unfurl.

Helped her to unfurl it.

And now he had led her, slowly yet masterfully, to this point. This moment. The moment she would take a life of her own, the apprentice becoming the expert in her own right.

She wasn't going to fail now.

"I remember this," Miley said, as if seized with a sudden inspiration. She turned back towards the doorway. "I remember now. I got it all confused in my head, but now I see it. I didn't go through the window – I went this way. I wrapped myself up in the sheet and I ran out of the door, right at him, because I thought that if he had a knife it would get caught up in the sheet and confuse him. And then I pushed it onto him, over his head, and just ran while he tried to get free of it."

"And he was caught up enough not to catch you?" Tara asked. There was a note of doubt in her voice. Miley had to do something about that.

"He stumbled and fell and got his feet tangled," Miley said, stepping forwards quicker and quicker as if she was retracing her own steps. "I went this way – right out through the door. And there was something… Something on the ground."

"What was it?" Tara asked.

"A shovel," Miley said. She looked around at her so-called helper. "There was a shovel. I think he was digging graves."

"Did you see where?" Tara asked. The eagerness in her eyes betrayed her. She wanted to know. She wanted to know so badly that she would take a stupid risk.

"I think so," Miley said, pointing out across the woods in the direction of what she knew would be the big lake. "I think it was out there." It was a breadcrumb, a morsel. Something so tempting that she didn't think the stupid Deputy Sheriff would be able to resist.

Of course, she knew where all of the graves were. She could lead this woman to every single one of them if she wanted to. But she only wanted to lead her to one.

To the empty one.

"If we're going into the trees, we should let someone know," Tara said. Miley cursed inwardly. Why did she have to be a stickler for the rules? "Just wait here. I'll put in a call." She grabbed her radio off her shoulder and started to talk into it, leaving Miley to stare out into the trees, her mind racing. What could she do? How could she manage to get out of this one? If there was a trail of evidence telling people where this Deputy Sheriff was, then it would be much easier to pin everything on Miley. She needed to be able to muddy the waters, to tell any story that would fit what she needed.

Maybe she would need to lead her further away from here, after all.

"Darn it." Tara muttered, letting wild hope flare for Miley. "There's no signal out here. I can't get a message through. I'll have to call them when we get back to clearer ground."

"That's okay," Miley nodded. "I'm okay."

Tara smiled encouragingly at her. "Right," she said. "Show me where you ran – let's find those graves."

"There were a few in a row," Miley said, taking off in the right direction. She went fairly quickly, thinking that it would be reasonable to think she was reenacting the past. "I was going fast – right through here. I'm sure it was this way."

"This fits with the direction you were coming from when you were found," Tara nodded.

"This way," Miley said, rushing off. She wanted to put Tara off guard. To make her run and stumble through the woods. Miley herself knew this area like the back of her hand. She had learned it on purpose, the knowledge useful should one of their girls ever really try to escape.

She only slowed down when they were in the thick of the woods, the place where no one would be able to find them unless they knew exactly where to look. And no one did.

"I think it was somewhere around here," Miley lied. "I'm not sure which way I went, though. Could you help me look?"

"Sure," Tara said. She took a few steps forward. "We can take a look together."

And she was still looking, really actually looking, when Miley grabbed the rock she had just stepped over and hit her over the head with it.

CHAPTER TWENTY SIX

Tara opened her eyes to a burning and throbbing pain in the back of her head.

It took seconds for things to come back to her, but those seconds hit her one after another like a sledgehammer. First she realized she was in the woods by the fact that she was looking up at trees. Then she remembered that she had come here with Miley as she caught sight of the survivor standing nearby. And finally – she recalled that the only person there with her, the only person who could possibly have hit her over the head, was Miley herself.

Tara tried to reach out to prop herself up so that she could sit, and found that she couldn't move her arms at all.

The final realization, the one that was a new fact rather than a memory, was that she was tied up. Her wrists and ankles were bound.

Miley had hit her over the head and tied her up.

"Oh! You're awake," Miley said. "Marvelous. I was hoping it wouldn't take you too long to wake up."

Tara looked at her, raising her head a little off the ground. It hurt, but not so much as to incapacitate her. "Why did you do that?" she asked.

It was more of a time-gaining exercise than anything. Tara was beginning to piece it all together well enough herself. There was only one reason why Miley would hit her over the head, knock her out, and then tie her up so that she couldn't run away.

It had to be because she wasn't a victim at all – and Tara had been fooled all along.

"Oh, by the way," Miley said. She moved behind Tara and then came back into view leaning over her, right before she forcibly pushed a gag over Tara's head and into her mouth. "We can't have you screaming, can we? Or asking a lot of annoying questions, either."

Miley stepped back and looked her over, as if proud of her handiwork.

"That's much better," Miley said. "You know, it was starting to get really annoying having to play along with you. You were soooo sympathetic. Sickening, really."

Was I supposed to be hard and cold towards an attempted murder victim? Tara thought. She couldn't say anything past the thick gag in her mouth, so she didn't even try. There would be time to test her boundaries – and expend her energy – once she thought she actually had a chance of getting away.

"Come on, then," Miley said. "What do you think? Have you figured it all out?"

Tara saw an opening, and she took it. She frowned, letting her eyes go blank and scared, as if she had no idea what was going on.

Miley smirked.

"Oh, why not tell you about it?" she asked. "As soon as we're done, I'll have to go back to pretending again and I won't be able to tell anyone about it. I won't even be able to tell Aric now that you've taken him in – unless that lawyer manages to get him off. But I really was quite clever, you know. Someone should know about it."

Tara said and did nothing, trying not to draw any attention to herself more than was necessary or to interrupt Miley. She wanted her to talk. In the meantime, she started moving her fingers behind her back as subtly as she could, trying to see if there was anything she could use – or any way she could get her hands free from the ropes.

"So, let's see. Well, Aric and I met three years ago. And yes, I was going to be one of his girls. You can tell because of the green eyes, can't you?" Miley preened for a moment, running a hand through her long red hair before tossing it back over her shoulders. "But it was… well, not love at first sight – recognition. We looked one another in the eyes and we just knew. We just knew that we were the same."

She sighed happily, as if she was recalling an especially fond memory – and then looked down at Tara for her reaction. Tara frowned, and tried to mumble something quietly through the gag, something that she hoped sounded like a question.

Her wandering fingers had found a rock. A flat panel of rock that had formed out of the earth, the rest of it buried under the soil and fallen leaves. Tara wasn't even sure it would have been visible if she was looking right at it, but her hands had found it. Now, if she could just shift towards it…

"By 'the same', I mean we're both killers, of course," Miley said. She gestured dismissively and began pacing up and down in front of Tara. "Except I soon realized we aren't the same, not really. I've helped him find girls to take. The last few, I even helped him lure them in so it wouldn't draw so much attention. No one thinks it's unusual when they see me hanging around a campsite or driving around town. It's not the same for Aric. When people see him, they talk about it. He couldn't risk that – that's why he always snatches them off the road or when they're on their own. I was able to speed up his process distinctly and get him a new girl whenever he wanted it – though of course he's always been cautious and likes to space them out."

She seemed to be rambling now, going on and on, lost in her own little world. Tara could tell she loved the sound of her own voice. Meanwhile, the whole time, Tara subtly tried to rub the edge of the rope that Miley had tied her up with against the edge of the rock she had found.

"Anyway, that's beside the point. I help him, you see. I help him tie them up and keep them and I watch while he does it. But it's not enough anymore. Aric – he's so cautious. So boring." She chuckled lightly. "I wanted to draw your attention off me, make myself look like a victim so you wouldn't arrest me. I was trying not to throw him under the bus, I swear. But now that you've taken him in… well, it's just so beautiful, isn't it? The police think the case is solved, I'll be able to fly back under the radar, and then… then I'll continue Aric's legacy, only I won't be so boring about it when I'm the one in control."

Tara had never wanted to be able to speak more in her life. She wanted to tell Miley that she would still get caught, that the police would be wary for years, that she would never get away with the same trick twice. She wanted to talk her out of this. But the gag was tight, and she knew there was no way she would be able to get out anything but an incoherent mumble. She worked on her ropes instead, praying that she would be able to get through them before Miley finished talking.

Miley looked down at her and Tara froze, not knowing whether she had been caught.

"What are you doing?" Miley asked.

Tara threw caution to the wind and started sawing her hands back and forth frantically, trying to get through the bonds as quickly as she could, knowing now that there was absolutely no time to lose.

Miley was on her again when Tara felt a pop, and her wrists flew apart.

It was too little, too late – but the same was true for Miley. The vicious redhead hadn't managed to get to Tara in time to totally pin her down, and the two of them wrestled against the ground for a moment before Tara managed to get enough strength to push hard against the other woman and roll to the side. She was away – but the relief only lasted a moment. Her ankles were still tied, her gag still in place, and there was nowhere for her to go.

Even if she had the time to scramble to her feet, she would fall right over again.

"Stop that," Miley told her crossly, and Tara had the feeling that she was someone who was used to getting her way. Someone who wasn't afraid to incur deadly consequences when she did not. She reached out - and grabbed Tara's blonde ponytail, dragging her backwards with a yank that made Tara want to scream.

She found herself laying on her back on the ground again, Miley over her. She knew this wasn't a fair fight and it wasn't something she could keep going forever. Miley had her hands free as well as her legs – she could move easier, run, jump, kick. All Tara was doing was keeping herself alive, and maybe not on a permanent basis.

She had to play dirty.

Tara reached up with her hands and scratched Miley's face on purpose, aiming for her eyes, feeling the slide of skin beneath her fingernails as she drew blood and made Miley shriek. The other woman jumped backwards, throwing herself clear of Tara and then glaring at her as Miley tried to shuffle herself backwards.

There wasn't time to get away, not really. There never had been.

Miley grabbed her by the joined ankles and pulled her back hard, and Tara's head bounced across the ground as she was dragged forward with no way to resist. Her hands skittered across the ground, seeking purchase, but all she could do was try to flail at Miley and attempt unsuccessfully to hit her.

"Hey!"

The shout ran out through the trees, making both Miley and Tara snap their heads in that direction. Tara scrambled backwards to take advantage of the moment while Miley got to her feet. Between the thick trunks of the trees, a flicker of movement caught Tara's attention – and then like a mirage coming into focus she realized she was looking at

Glenn, his Sheriff's uniform providing excellent camouflage against the trees and the rocky terrain.

Tara wanted to yell something – to tell Glenn where she was, to warn him, to let him know to watch out. But her mouth was still gagged. She tried to scream and only succeeded in making a loud noise which contained no words, no meaning. Glenn glanced in her direction.

And Miley charged at him, holding a rock raised over her head in both hands.

Tara's eyes bugged open for a moment and then she looked away, concentrating on rolling so that she could get up. She heard – half-felt – the thud of the impact when the rock in Miley's hand connected with Glenn. The distraction she had provided had left him with no time to react, no ability to defend himself. There was no time to dwell on what she should or shouldn't have done. There was only the now and what she needed to do next to fix this.

Tara didn't leave herself time to think beyond taking action. She managed to get up and shuffle one step, two steps, fighting to keep her balance against the odds – and then she lunged, throwing herself through the air towards Miley. She landed against the other woman with enough force to knock her down before she could hit Glenn again, and she landed with a heavy thump. Tara went down on top of her, unable to keep her balance.

"Get her hands!" Glenn shouted, and Tara grabbed her hands in the moment when Miley was winded and incapable of getting away, and Glenn threw himself down with the handcuffs to snap them onto her wrists.

And Tara breathed – because they had done it.

Miley struggled against her cuffs for a moment and then went limp. Tara looked up at the red welt forming on Glenn's right cheek that was probably about to evolve into a black eye, and she saw him eyeing the side of her head where she no doubt had some kind of lump as evidence of her own blow.

She gave an exhausted chuckle, a sound of pure relief, and Glenn joined her – and then reached for his radio to call it in.

CHAPTER TWENTY SEVEN

Tara slumped into the chair opposite Sheriff Braddock's desk, glad that this time she wasn't about to take another verbal beating. Glenn sat carefully in the chair next to her, holding his head at a weird angle – he'd taken to moving strangely now that he couldn't see out of one eye very well.

"Jesus," Sheriff Braddock said, staring at the two of them. "You look like you went ten rounds in the ring with each other."

"Not each other," Tara pointed out. "But otherwise, that feels pretty accurate."

"Well, either way," Braddock said. "You two did very well. Rosalyn Clement has been discharged from the hospital and sent home – she's perfectly fine. You saved her life. And you, Glenn, also saved the life of a fellow officer."

"I had it handled," Tara joked, looking at Glenn sideways.

"She probably did," Glenn admitted.

"You need to be prepared to testify in court in Miley Piper's trial," Braddock carried on. "Particularly you, Tara. Her confession to you is apparently the only one she's willing to give, although we'll have to keep trying to push her. Meanwhile, as soon as he heard that she had been arrested, Aric Cordell has given us a full confession that excludes Miley from his narrative – as if she wasn't involved at all."

"Do you think she's going to get away with it?" Tara frowned with concern.

"We have her on assault, and I think we can get her on attempted murder just for what she did to you," Braddock said. "The courts will decide whether she can be tried for being his accomplice. I think she will be. Then it's down to a jury."

Tara's mouth was dry as she thought about how good a liar Miley was. How she had fooled her easily.

"She'll be going away, though," Glenn pointed out. "No matter what. You don't assault two deputies and just walk free."

"Oh, she'll be away for a long time," Braddock confirmed. "And if the first trial doesn't stick, we'll appeal the results and get another one. Don't worry, Tara. She won't be out to attack anyone else."

Tara nodded, looking down at her hands. She wished they hadn't been able to figure out what she was worried about so easily. She shifted in her seat. She was a Deputy Sheriff – she wasn't supposed to be worried about her own personal safety, just that of the citizens she was sworn to protect. "I'm glad she won't be able to try to kill again," she said, which was a neutral proposition and therefore far more comfortable.

"I want both of you to go home and get some rest," Sheriff Braddock said. "You've earned it. We'll recuperate, debrief, and then carry on as normal. The job doesn't wait, but the rest of us can pick up the slack and work on finding those other bodies for a few days."

"Thank you," Tara murmured, her sentiments echoed by Glenn. "I'll be back to work in two days."

"Make it three," Braddock said, giving her a stern look. "You were in personal danger today, Deputy Sheriff. I don't want you working yourself so hard you don't recover."

Tara nodded silently, unable to really agree to something she didn't want to commit to. She figured in two days she'd creep back into the station and see if he noticed.

"Alright, get out of here," Sheriff Braddock grinned. "And go the back way. I'm handling the press conference in ten minutes so you don't have to."

That earned another and much more heartfelt round of thanks as Tara and Glenn stood up. They left the Sheriff's office together, gathered their things from their desks, and found themselves walking to the exit at the same time as well.

"How's your eye?" Tara asked. She looked sideways at Glenn, trying not to wince. The whole of his right eye was more or less one swollen mass. "Can you actually drive with that thing?"

"Yeah, I'll be fine," Glenn said. He turned to go towards his car and walked right into a railing that had presumably been in his blind spot.

"Really?" Tara asked flatly.

"Uh," Glenn hesitated. "Could you give me a lift home?"

"Right answer," Tara said, patting him on the arm. "Come on. It's this way." She hooked her arm over his elbow as if he was escorting her and led him to her car. The connection between them felt warm and nice, companionable. Like they should walk around that way all the time. Which was ridiculous, given the nature of their job.

"Thanks," Glenn said sheepishly, reaching for the handle of the passenger side door as Tara reluctantly let go of him to walk around to the other side. They got in next to one another and Tara started the car, looking over her shoulder to back out of the space and make her way out of the parking lot.

"Will you be okay without your car tomorrow?" she asked.

Glenn shrugged. "When I next need it, I'll just walk back," he said.

"Only when you've rested up," Tara warned him. She sounded like Braddock. And a hypocrite, she knew.

"Yes, ma'am," Glenn said, and Tara glanced sideways to see him grinning.

"I'm glad she didn't..." she started, and then stopped herself.

"Kill me?" Glenn suggested.

Tara grimaced. "Yes, but I didn't want to say it," she said. "It's kind of morbid, isn't it?"

"A little. But I'm glad, too," Glenn said. There was a pause, then he began a rambling explanation. "I mean, I'm glad that she didn't kill you. Not that I'm *not* glad she didn't kill me, you know, obviously I am, I just..."

"We're both glad," Tara said, offering some rescue.

"Right," Glenn chuckled. He glanced at her, and she could feel his eyes on her. "Tara, I..."

"What?" she asked. He didn't respond, so when she had to pause at an intersection's red light, she turned to look at him.

Strangely, he blushed and looked out of the window. "Nothing," he said. "Just, thanks."

"Thanks, yourself," Tara said. "I wouldn't have been able to save you if you hadn't saved me first."

"I guess we're even," Glenn said.

"We're even," Tara agreed.

She drove in silence the rest of the way to Glenn's house, dropped him off with a wave and a promise to check in tomorrow so they both knew the other was still doing well, and then carried on driving back home.

The problem was that as soon as she was alone, thoughts started to crowd in on her.

She'd saved Rosalyn Clement. She had. She'd had help, obviously, but – saving someone's life felt so good. More than that: she had seen firsthand how worried Todd Tatton had been when his girlfriend didn't return home. Rosalyn's parents, any siblings she might have had, her friends and colleagues at work – all of them would have felt that worry, too.

Tara knew that worry all too well. She had lived it.

And now she had been able to take that worry away for Rosalyn's family and friends, and give them back their hope. She had given them back Rosalyn, in one piece and alive, and she knew how much that would mean to them.

She knew how much it would have meant to her.

And in that instant, in the fantasy of that relief, she knew that she wanted it. She wanted it so badly that she was prepared, at last, to accept the outcome either way. Even if she only found out that her sister was dead and had been dead for ten years, it would be a welcome relief.

No more guessing. No more dreaming. No more wondering and tossing and turning through nightmares.

Tara was going to reopen her sister's case.

She paused outside her home, turning off the car's engine but making no move to get out. Doing this would cause a lot of pain to people that she loved. Her mother and father lived their lives almost in a state of willful ignorance, setting the place for Cassie as if she was about to walk back through the door but never actually talking about her. Jessy held this belief in her head that she would have been able to find Cassie if she had been Sheriff back then, and to go behind her back to investigate it would only deepen the rift between her and Tara.

Even Sheriff Braddock would think she was testing his authority, doubting that he had done a good job back then. And Glenn would be swept up in that, too. Glenn would want to investigate with her, she knew that, but she couldn't let him risk getting involved in Braddock's ire.

She had been afraid for a long time that Braddock really had missed something. She believed in her mentor – believed he had done everything he could. But if she reopened the case and found that he had missed something…

The pain it would cause her didn't matter. Her sister was more important than Sheriff Braddock, even with everything the older man had done for her and her career. Cassie was the most important thing, and Tara didn't know why it had taken her this long to see it.

She would do this quietly. Secretly. Make it her mission to discover as much as she could without arousing suspicion. And only when she was sure she had something would she pursue it openly and find a resolution to the case.

Tara was going to find her little sister, and suddenly she knew without a doubt in her heart that absolutely nothing was going to stop her until she succeeded.

GIRL WITHOUT A HOME
(A Tara Strong Mystery—Book 2)

When a body is discovered high up in a remote mountain cave, Deputy Sheriff Tara Strong quickly realizes she has a serial killer on her hands. In a race against time, Tara must comb the hundreds of caves in an endless mountain range to stop the killer before he outwits her and claims his next victim.

"A brilliant book. I couldn't put it down and I never guessed who the murderer was!"
—Reader review for Only Murder

GIRL WITHOUT A HOME is book #2 in a new series by #1 bestselling and critically acclaimed mystery and suspense author Rylie Dark, whose books have received over 2,000 five-star reviews and ratings.

Tara Strong has risen to become her county's Deputy Sheriff through her bravery and her brilliant capacity to enter a killer's minds. Small-town life in the mountains, centered around their picturesque lake, should be idyllic. But Tara has already seen enough to know that there is a dark side to everything, that small towns hide secrets, that everyone has something in their past—and that a killer may just be lurking right next door.

Tara remains haunted by her own past, by her missing sister, by her guilt over the unsolved case. She must battle the demons of her own past, while trying to get ahead in a male-dominated police force.

Can Tara keep it together long enough to catch a killer?

A cat-and-mouse thriller with harrowing twists and turns and filled with heart-pounding suspense, the TARA STRONG mystery series offers a fresh twist on the genre as it introduces two brilliant protagonists who will make you fall in love and keep you turning pages late into the night.

Future books in this series are also available.

"I loved this thriller, read it in one sitting. Lots of twists and turns and I didn't guess the
culprit at all… Already pre-ordered the second!"
—Reader review for Only Murder

"This book takes off with a bang… An excellent read, and I'm looking forward to the next book!"
—Reader review for SEE HER RUN

"Fantastic book! It was hard to put down. I can't wait to see what happens next!"
—Reader review for SEE HER RUN

"The twists and turns kept coming. Can't wait to read the next book!"
—Reader review for SEE HER RUN

"A must-read if you enjoy action-packed stories with good plots!"
—Reader review for SEE HER RUN

"I really like this author and this series starts with a bang. It will keep you turning the pages till the end of the book and wanting more."
—Reader review for SEE HER RUN

"I can't say enough about this author! How about 'out of this world'! This author is going to go far!"
—Reader review for ONLY MURDER

Rylie Dark

Bestselling author Rylie Dark is author of the SADIE PRICE FBI SUSPENSE THRILLER series, comprising six books (and counting); of the CARLY SEE FBI SUSPENSE THRILLER series, comprising six books (and counting); of the MIA NORTH FBI SUSPENSE THRILLER series, comprising six books (and counting); of the MORGAN STARK FBI SUSPENSE THRILLER series, comprising five books (and counting); of the HAILEY ROCK FBI SUSPENSE THRILLER series, comprising five books (and counting); and of the TARA STRONG MYSTERY series, comprising five books (and counting).

An avid reader and lifelong fan of the mystery and thriller genres, Rylie loves to hear from you, so please feel free to visit www.ryliedark.com to learn more and stay in touch.

BOOKS BY RYLIE DARK

TARA STRONG MYSTERY
GIRL WITHOUT A CHANCE (Book #1)
GIRL WITHOUT A HOME (Book #2)
GIRL WITHOUT A TRACE (Book #3)
GIRL WITHOUT A NAME (Book #4)
GIRL WITHOUT A PRAYER (Book #5)

HAILEY ROCK FBI SUSPENSE THRILLER
BEHIND YOU (Book #1)
BESIDE YOU (Book #2)
AFTER YOU (Book #3)
WATCHING YOU (Book #4)
JUDGING YOU (Book #5)

SADIE PRICE FBI SUSPENSE THRILLER
ONLY MURDER (Book #1)
ONLY RAGE (Book #2)
ONLY HIS (Book #3)
ONLY ONCE (Book #4)
ONLY SPITE (Book #5)
ONLY MADNESS (Book #6)

MIA NORTH FBI SUSPENSE THRILLER
SEE HER RUN (Book #1)
SEE HER HIDE (Book #2)
SEE HER SCREAM (Book #3)
SEE HER VANISH (Book #4)
SEE HER GONE (Book #5)
SEE HER DEAD (Book #6)

CARLY SEE FBI SUSPENSE THRILLER
NO WAY OUT (Book #1)
NO WAY BACK (Book #2)

NO WAY HOME (Book #3)
NO WAY LEFT (Book #4)
NO WAY UP (Book #5)
NO WAY TO DIE (Book #6)

MORGAN STARK FBI SUSPENSE THRILLER
TOO LATE (Book #1)
TOO CLOSE (Book #2)
TOO FAR GONE (Book #3)
TOO LOST (Book #4)
TOO BROKEN (Book #5)

Made in the USA
Monee, IL
05 December 2023

48181988R00100